defend...
the ball to Roy
well in amongst   ...hen
mistake. Roy was cutting...

'The wing!' yelled the keeper. 'Watch out for the one–two.'

Defenders span for Roy, but *too late*! – the return pass was already over their heads.

Starting to come out, the keeper had a change of heart; he fell back and crouched low. The ball was dropping. Lee stretched his stride the last few steps – it would have to be on the left foot. Leaning to the right, he hooked the ball with the full force of the through-sweep – perfect!

'*GOAL!*'

BROOKSIE

NEIL ARKSEY

CORGI YEARLING BOOKS

BROOKSIE
A CORGI YEARLING BOOK : 0 440 863813

First publication in Great Britain

PRINTING HISTORY
Corgi Yearling edition published 1998

Set in 13/15pt New Century Schoolbook by
Phoenix Typesetting, Ilkley, West Yorkshire

Corgi Yearling Books are published by
Transworld Publishers Ltd,
61–63 Uxbridge Road, Ealing, London W5 5SA,
in Australia by Transworld Publishers (Australia) Pty. Ltd,
15–25 Helles Avenue, Moorebank, NSW 2170,
and in New Zealand by Transworld Publishers (NZ) Ltd,
3 William Pickering Drive, Albany, Auckland.

Made and printed in Great Britain by
Cox & Wyman Ltd, Reading, Berkshire.

For – Katie, Mumcat, Thumpy and Sweep

Thanks – Carob, Pia, Val and The Gnome;
Elizabeth, Margaret and the gang;
and everyone who encouraged.

CHAPTER 1

Match Postponed

Lee Brooks kicked the bench. What a pathetic first half! He'd been worse than useless. Again.

'Right! Gather round and listen.' Mr MacKay glared and puffed out his big chest. 'In case you'd all forgotten – this is the final.'

Lee tried to focus on Mr MacKay's words, tried to concentrate.

'We've had our ups,' said Mr MacKay, 'and this season, Lord help us, we've had our downs. But it's the end of the school year and we're here!' He whacked his palm against a locker. 'That's of no consequence if we fail to score in the next thirty-five minutes. To take home that cup we need *goals.*'

Sheepish nods all round.

'Over in the other changing room,' said Mr MacKay, 'their coach is probably saying the exact same thing, so bear in mind – we need *more goals than them.*'

More nods and murmurs.

'Brooks . . .'

Lee bit his lip. Everyone looked down at the floor; they knew what was coming.

'. . . same thing I've been nagging you about all term.' Mr MacKay's tone softened slightly. 'I know you've had a lot on your mind . . .'

Slight understatement! Lee nodded. 'Yes, sir.'

'. . . especially today, with your father so much in the spotlight . . .'

Dad's first game in months. Last game of the season. Last chance.

'. . . but that doesn't alter the fact that out there,' Mr MacKay pointed towards the pitch, 'you are *part of a team.*'

'Yes, sir.' Lee glanced at the clock. Dad would be on the pitch.

Mr MacKay stepped away from the lockers. Plastered flat, his dark hair accentuated his beady eyes and mean mouth.

'*Brooks*,' he snapped, 'the midfield drop back because of *you*.'

'Yes, sir.'

'. . . you're not *reading* the game . . .'

Lee stared at his chewed fingernails, at the mud on his boots. He was letting them down. He'd been letting them down all term. He must *concentrate*.

'We know you can do it, Brooks . . .'

From behind his fringe, Lee caught the pitying glances of his teammates.

'A midfield playmaker creates opportunities: left, right and centre. Am I right?'

'Yes, sir.'

'If I didn't believe you could recover the magnificent form you displayed in the first few months of the season, I'd have replaced you by now.' The frown deepened. 'This half, I want your mind one-hundred-and-ten-per-cent on the game. Can you do it?'

'Yes, sir.'

Mr MacKay's piercing eyes stared long and hard. 'Right!' he said suddenly. 'Good! Now . . . the rest applies to everybody – we're getting the balls, but we're losing them.' He made a fist. '*Maintain* possession. *Push* forward. Keep them on the back foot.' He punched the air. 'Get out there and *GIVE IT TO THEM*!'

The team jumped up from the benches and shook their fists. '*Lyndhurst! Lyndhurst! Lyndhurst* . . .' They stomped their boots on the tiles.

Here and there, Lee caught a wink or a nod. As they crowded towards the door, hands patted his back.

'One last thing . . .' Mr MacKay barred the door with his arm. 'The Brooks family have had something of a tough time these last few months, maintaining their privacy from newspapers and TV. The groundsman's on the gate, we shouldn't have trouble with prying eyes, but just in case . . . out there—' Mr MacKay nodded towards the pitch, '– make sure you only use Lee's first name.'

'Lee!' A flash of white – Walton on the wing, pony-tail flapping in the breeze.

Lee looked ahead. One, two, *three* red shirts were closing in for the kill. He cut left, accelerating round them. Defenders fell back.

Stocky Reeves was in the clear just ahead. Price, with his long legs, cruised up easily on the inside.

'Lee!'

He flicked it up and over.

They had them on the run. Time to retake the middle.

'Take it all the way!' yelled Mr MacKay from the touchline.

Lee pulled in behind Price. Putting on a spurt, Price was heading for the opening.

'*Price!*' Lee yelled. '*Man on!*'

Too late. Price was down.

'*Ref!*' yelled Mr MacKay. 'Where are your *eyes*?'

The ref signalled: play on.

Lee took off with the ball, passed to Reeves and moved up.

Reeves chipped it straight back. *Nifty*.

Reds swooped from all sides. Lee swerved hard right.

'*Go on!*' screeched Mr MacKay.

Lee cut across the goalmouth. Walton was running in. This was it! Fancy footwork time. Draw the defence.

'*Go on, lad!*'

Lee danced. Defenders harried. He zigzagged. Flipped it. Accelerated round to collect and chipped it straight to Walton's boot.

'*YES!*'

What a . . . save*?!* What a *keeper*! A shot like that!

Lee headed back to his own half.

A pat on the back. 'Nice try!'

Lyndhurst's goalkeeper bounced the ball and studied the field, giving his players a chance to move forward.

Lee ran into position, turned and trotted backwards.

He stopped. There was *that feeling* again – everyone watching him, waiting for him to mess up. He rubbed his neck and looked round.

At the edge of the playing field, over by the fence, something glinted in the sun.

'Come on, Lyndhurst! Come on, Lyndhurst!' Mr MacKay led the parents in a chant.

Lee craned his neck. Soaring overhead, the ball dropped deep into the Lyndhurst half.

Red forwards charged.

But Fat Pat got to it, easily. He fed it out to Morris. Morris had buckets of room . . . the reds were on the wrong foot.

Lee put on a spurt – action time again!

Something flashed over by the fence. *Ignore it!* he told himself. Concentrate *one-hundred-and-ten-per-cent!* Don't let Lyndhurst down!

Walton was on the wing and Morris on the inside. Lee took the middle. Reeves was up front, Price and Thorpe slightly behind to the left. A line of whites pushing forward, with Lee in the middle.

'Take it *all the way*!' yelled Mr MacKay.

They crossed the halfway line.

Walton passed inside.

Morris broke formation, veering in sharply towards the centre.

Sunlight flashed again. Suddenly, Lee stumbled, stared and froze; from behind the fence, a long *camera lens* was pointing towards the pitch.

'What are you *playing at*?' roared Mr MacKay.

Lee jerked round. He felt sick; his legs were shaking.

Morris and Price were down. Reeves was surrounded.

Lee clutched his stomach, rubbed his legs and tried to run.

Behind the goal, parents were turning away from the game, towards the car park.

Squinting into the sun, Lee could just make out a group of figures running on to the playing field. They were heading for the pitch . . . their movements were strangely lop-sided . . . they were carrying *cameras*!

'Pass!'

Lee turned back to the game. Blood boomed in his ears; Walton was waving and yelling for all he was worth. Reeves had been tackled. The ball had rolled loose.

Lee sprinted for it . . . misjudged it . . . and went sprawling.

He scrambled to his feet. He still had the ball. Everybody – players on both sides, the parents, the ref – *everybody* was staring at the advancing photographers, as they bobbed and lurched their way towards the goal.

Mr MacKay was pointing and yelling, as if to shoo them away.

'Brooksie! Man on!'

Lee twisted.

Down on one knee, photographers pointed their huge lenses across the pitch.

He twisted again.

Again – photographers raised their cameras, giant eyes homing in on their target.

There was nowhere to run. He took a deep breath. There was nothing else for it . . .

He charged for the touchline. Players from both sides stared as he flew past. With a little skip, he back-heeled the ball just short of touch and kept on going –

right into the group of onlooking parents.

'Brooksie!'

'Lee!'

'Brooksie!'

The photographers, now certain of their target, closed in. Hunters with big guns, they pointed their lenses into the small crowd. The whir, whine and click of cameras began.

CHAPTER 2

Departure

Fingers in ears, Lee sat on the toilet. Frantic voices, arguing and shouting, filled the air around him. Bodies banged against the cubicle door; feet scuffled.

He stared at the back of the door. His sprint for the pavilion, pursued by photographers, two teams, Mr MacKay, the ref and parents, must have looked *ridiculous*.

'Lee!'

The noise had quietened.

'Lee, it's OK – it's all right now . . .' Mr MacKay's usually gruff voice had softened a tinge. 'Lee – the police are here. The photographers and reporters are all locked outside – it's OK, you can come out now.'

He couldn't. His knees were shaking,

he was trembling. He couldn't move or speak.

'Lee!'

He looked up.

An anxious, straining face appeared in the gap above the top of the cubicle.

Midge Morris grinned. 'Soon have you out!' Scrambling over the top, he dropped down inside and unlocked the door.

Behind the door – gawping faces.

Mr MacKay leant down. One of his eyes was swollen. 'Don't worry lad,' he whispered, 'you're all right now – you're safe!'

Lee felt himself being lifted to his feet. 'The boy needs air!' yelled Mr MacKay, half-dragging, half-carrying him out of the cubicle. 'He needs AIR!'

Cameras flashed, clicked and whirred. Shielding him, Mr MacKay and a policeman pushed and barged a path through photographers and reporters.

'Lee . . .'

'*Lee!*'

'A few words about your father?'

'Come on – Lee!'

'*Lee* – still proud of your dad?'

'What about today's performance, eh?'

'*Lee!*'

'How's things at home?'

'Your mum and dad – do they argue? Do they fight?'

Shouting and jostling, photographers and reporters thrust tape-recorders, microphones and cameras over heads, under arms – through any gap they could find in the line of police.

Inside the car, behind the protection of darkened windows, Mum hugged him. 'You all right?'

He nodded.

The car sped off.

'You're safe now.' Mum pushed back his fringe. 'They lost . . . Dad was sent off.'

'Mrs Brooks! Mrs Brooks – *what now?*'

'Mrs Brooks!'

'What's going on at home, Mrs Brooks?'

'Lee!'

Reporters and photographers blocked the entrance to the drive. Police struggled to push them back.

'Mrs Brooks!'

'*Lee* . . . How d'you feel about your dad now – Lee?'

'Mrs Brooks . . . Come on! Just a few words – tell us your thoughts on Brooksie's recent pitch behaviour?'

18

'How's Brooksie treating *you*, Mrs Brooks?'

Cameras flashed, pressed against the darkened glass. Instinctively, Lee raised his arm to shield his face. Mum did the same.

The car slowed to a crawl. The police were fighting a losing battle. The gravel driveway seemed to stretch into a long winding road. Reaching the house took for ever.

'*Lee!*'

'Where do you go from here, Mrs Brooks?'

'Mrs Brooks – things must be fraught in the Brooks household?'

'They call you "Brooksie" don't they, Lee? What's that like?'

'How are things between you and your husband, Mrs Brooks?'

'Lee – what about your dad? What d'you make of it all?'

'Like father, like son, is it, Lee?'

'Come on! Just a few words?'

'A few words, Mrs Brooks – come *on*!'

'What's he like at home?'

The front door was opened by a policeman. Lee and Mum dashed inside.

In the hall, little Tanya and two big policemen were waiting with the suitcases, playing I-Spy . . .

Lee opened his eyes and peered at his reflection in the window; it was little more than a dark shadow, but he knew how he must look. He felt exhausted; the skin around his eyes was sore from tears and rubbing.

He twisted round. On the back seat, Tanya slept peacefully curled-up.

Taking one hand off the wheel, Mum pushed back her bob and rubbed her neck. She glanced and smiled. Little half-moon dimples appeared in her cheeks like brackets round her mouth – the best smile in the world.

'You all right?'

Lee nodded.

'Not long now.'

It had still been light when they'd set off. Now, streets he didn't recognize flashed past, lit up by shop signs and amber lights.

'Dad needs some time on his own,' said Mum. 'He's got some difficult decisions to make.'

They were going to stay at her friend

Cherelle's for a while. Cherelle was away; the flat needed looking-after.

'What's it going to be like?' said Lee.

'Well . . .' said Mum, '. . . first and foremost – it'll be pest-free. No more photographers. No more journalists.' She glanced across. 'We're going to be incognito.'

'Cognito?' muttered Lee.

Mum chuckled. 'Invisible, then. In disguise. No false beards or any of that palaver. At least – not for the time being. But, from now on, we're going to be *Mansfields*.'

Lee stared. *Mansfield* was her name before she married. 'Are you and Dad getting divorced?'

'No, darling.' Mum glanced back at his sister. 'Things aren't quite as drastic as that . . .' She squeezed his hand. '. . . though I may have to get a job – something part-time . . .'

'What else?' said Lee. 'You said "first and foremost" . . .'

Mum nodded. 'There's a pitch to practice and play on.'

Lee scowled and twisted to face the window.

'I thought you'd be pleased,' said Mum.

Lee pressed his face against the glass. There was a horrible bitter-sour taste in his mouth. He was never usually car-sick, but now – his stomach was churning. He pulled his feet up on to the seat and tucked his knees into his chest. 'I've been useless all term,' he mumbled. 'I don't have what it takes. Today was the last straw.'

'Nonsense!' said Mum. 'You can't be expected to perform at your best all the time. It's been a difficult year . . .' She glanced across. '. . . and *a particularly trying day*.'

He groaned.

'Don't be so hard on yourself,' said Mum.

He could feel his bottom lip trembling. He bit it. '*I hate football*,' he said, spitting the words.

'Of course,' said Mum.

'I'm done with the stupid game,' he snapped.

Keeping her eyes on the road, Mum gave a little nod. 'We'll see.'

CHAPTER 3

Fresh Start

Brown fog swirls. He's zig-zagging, first one way then the other, between shadowy figures. They snarl and grunt. They clutch and swipe. Their eyes glare.

Above him, the sky smokes and glows like embers. He's running; there's a ball at his feet. His stride lengthens. The dark shapes howl and give chase.

They're closing in.

He dodges, he gathers pace . . . he ducks, jerks, swerves . . . he charges full pelt through the darkness. The darkness shakes and roars in his wake. He's getting there . . . *he's getting there* . . .

He's going to make it . . .

A huge creature, monstrous ugly, with

the girth and *smell* of a bull, churns through the fog towards him. The fog boils. The bull-man snorts and twists, and with a single scything kick *flings* himself . . .

Blinking open his eyes, Lee gasped for breath. He was shaking and sweating – his heart jumping in his chest.

Relax.

Suddenly, there was pain – a *murderous* pain, stabbing his calf.

Digging his thumbs into the muscle, he forced himself to press hard and deep. '*Unnnnngggh . . .!*' He bit the pillow, half-groaning, half-shrieking.

'*Unnnnnnngh . . . aaaagggh!*'

The cramp had faded.

Exhausted, he massaged sleep from his face.

Early-morning sun glared through a crack in the curtains; it lasered across the ceiling just above his head. He glanced around at the poky room; the clock on the wall said: quarter-to-six.

'Lee?'

Tanya shifted on the bunk below.

'Lee – you talk in your sleep.'

'You shouldn't be awake.'

'You were mumbling and fidgeting *all* night . . .'

'Tanya – it's not even six. Back to sleep.'

'. . . and you yelled stuff . . .'

'If you say so – now *sleep*.'

Lee lay absolutely still, listening to Tanya's struggle to get comfortable. Gradually, her fidgeting grew less. It stopped. Her breathing became slow and rhythmical . . . she was asleep.

The nightmare was still fresh. Reaching back past the pillows, Lee lifted the curtain and squinted. In the yard below, a car spluttered and pulled away from its parking space. He watched till it was out of sight.

He lifted further. It had been dark when they'd arrived last night. This was his new world: gloomy brown-grey blocks four stories high. Not what he was used to – no big house, no massive garden, no *grass* even. Just cracked tarmac and tired-looking cars.

He folded his arms behind his head and closed his eyes. Not to sleep, or dream. To *recall*.

He pictured a 'B'. Then an 'R'. Letter by letter, he formed the word 'BROOKSIE' in his head, in large bold capitals.

He felt his lips tighten in a smile. *That* was Dad. Another headline arrived:

FIVE! — BRILLIANT BROADSIDE
FROM STEVE BROOKS

That was Dad, too.

From somewhere between his chest and belly, a warmth spread out towards his head and toes.

BROOKSIE BRINGS IT HOME

He could dredge up every headline word-for-word; every picture too — back pages and front. Some of the articles he'd read so many times, he knew chunks of them off-by-heart:

'*. . . no mistaking the man-of-the-match for this Wembley crowd — Steve 'Brooksie' Brooks. Year after year, he comes up with the goods; today was no exception. This afternoon, with one resounding roar, the crowd hailed their hero again and again and again . . .*'

From the bunk below came a quiet muttering-mewing noise. Tanya shifted her position, lay still for a moment, then made the sound again.

BRUTAL BREAK FOR BROOKSIE

Lee flinched – felt himself stiffen. He took a deep breath . . .

'. . . *it could be several months before England's most consistently brilliant player is able to take part in any training. Over the years, Steve Brooks has been luckier than most in the injury stakes, but recovery times for this type of break can be lengthy. Don't expect to see him playing before next year . . .*'

No! He wanted to shout out. This wasn't what he'd meant to recall. He clutched the duvet to his chin.

CONVALESCING BROOKSIE PILES ON THE POUNDS

BOOZING BROOKSIE?

He pulled the pillow down over his face.

BROOKSIE'S SAD DECLINE

BROOKSIE – FINISHED?

Eyes open, or shut – it made no difference: the headlines now had a momentum of their own . . .

'Lee?'

'What now?'

'You were making the bed shake.'

'Tanya . . .' Lee peered at the clock. Seven-thirty! He must have dropped off!

Brown curls, then the face of a six-year-old pixie appeared at the top of the ladder. Tanya smiled, irritatingly. 'Yes, *Leeee*?'

'*Yes, Leeee* . . .' he mimicked.

'You!' Pulling a face, Tanya raised a fist.

Lee grabbed it and made an uglier face in return. He knew he shouldn't sink to her level but . . .

Drrrrrrrng!

The loud, unfamiliar sound made both of them jump.

Drrrrrrrng!

The doorbell rang again. Lee and Tanya stared at each other.

Drrrrrrrng!

Tanya squealed and giggled, she jabbed a mocking finger at Lee with her free hand. 'You jumped,' she said. *'Scaredeeee!'*

Suddenly, she had twisted free and was scrambling down the ladder.

Drrrrrrrng!

Lee swung over the side of the bunk.

Already Tanya had the bedroom door open. Squeaking with excitement, she scuttled into the corridor.

He gave chase.

Drrrrrrrng!

He could see the accident coming before it happened. Squealing like a pig, Tanya glanced back as she raced down the corridor. He yelled too late. Crashing into a small shelf, Tanya lost her balance and fell.

On the edge of the shelf a china cat teetered and dropped. Lee flung himself twisting through the air and over the body of his sister.

'Ouch!' As his head whacked the radiator his hand grasped the coldness of the cat.

Drrrrrrrrng! Mum dashed from her room, threw him an angry look and hurried to the door.

'Nice save, Lee!' sniggered Tanya. 'Perhaps you should try being a goalie!'

'Very funny,' he grunted.

'Knock-down ginger!' yelled Mum, '. . . on our first Sunday morning – thanks for the welcome!'

The front door slammed.

Mum reappeared, glowering. 'After all yesterday's stress,' she growled, '*I* need a lie in. Complete hush – till ten – *understood*?'

CHAPTER 4

Kick-about

'They're waving!' said Tanya, waving back. 'Don't you want to go and meet them?'

'No,' snapped Lee.

'They're boys,' said Tanya. 'They look your age . . .'

'You can't see.'

'Well they *sound* your age,' said Tanya, 'and they've got a football!'

'So?'

'So – you're football *crazy*; you can never resist a kick-about.'

'How would *you* know . . .?'

Lee squinted against the sun. He could just make out three figures – two tall, one short. They were whistling and shouting as they sauntered across the yard. The short one pointed up at the window. Was he beckoning . . . or making some other gesture?

'Tanya,' said Lee firmly. 'Back to bed.'

'You,' she snapped, 'you go back to bed.'

Lee shook his head. 'I'm going out.'

'See!' said Tanya. 'I *knew* you would.'

'Just for a wander – to recce the place.'

'To what?'

'You know – look about.'

Tanya grinned. 'I'm coming too.'

'You can't.'

'That's not fair . . .'

Putting a finger to his lips, Lee gagged his sister with his other hand. 'Sorry,' he said, '– but that's the way it works.'

Tanya struggled and tried to bite him.

He tightened his grip, gently. 'Listen,' he said, 'because I'm older, I get the blame for anything we do – *that's* not fair.' He loosened his hand.

Tanya pouted.

'I won't be long,' he said.

Lee crept past Mum's bedroom to the front door. The latch was stiff, the letterbox rattled and the door squeaked on its hinges. He held his breath – listening for signs of stirring.

Then he was out, along the walkway and into the dingy stairwell. He flew down the stairs three and four at a time, past graffiti and a strong smell of wee.

Up at the window, his sister pulled her ugliest face. Squat blocks of flats surrounded the yard; it was crammed with cars and flower-beds – choking with rubbish. There was no sign of the boys, but from a road between the blocks he could hear laughter and a ball skittering back and forth.

Waving to Tanya, he set off at a jog.

Blocks of garages stretched in both directions. The boys were some way off.

He put on a spurt. 'Hey!'

They halted and turned, watching him come.

He slowed to a walk.

The tallest one was black. His legs were *long*. Digging his trainer under the ball, the boy flipped it into the air.

An Indian-looking boy with a top-knot caught the ball on his chest. He balanced the ball on his instep, let it roll, then punted it high.

The third boy was white, shorter than the other two; his fair hair was straggly, his clothes scruffy. 'Look who it is!' he yelled, catching the ball on his foot. 'We saw you arrive last night. Hope the doorbell didn't spoil anyone's lie-in!'

Lee shrugged.

Flipping the ball high above his head, the short scruffy boy tapped himself on the chest. 'Dent!' he yelled. He stared at Lee, never once glancing up at the ball.

Lee stared back. Was this a challenge? Or an offer of friendship?

The ball dropped straight to the boy's foot. *'Yours!'* he yelled.

The volley came at Lee like a rocket – *right for his face*. He jumped, reacting without thinking, and caught it full-force on the chest.

Whump!

He staggered, the ball tumbled to his feet. With one glance, he *whacked* it straight back. *'Yours!'* he yelled. His target jack-knifed to the ground.

Lee hurried over.

Dent lay sprawled in front of a stack of full bin-bags, his two companions standing over him. He scrambled to his feet, kicking at a heap of spilled rubbish. 'They should clean this place up!' he snapped. 'It's dangerous.' He glowered at his two companions – they were smirking. 'I *tripped*!'

he snarled, daring them to contradict.

They nodded, trying to hide their smiles.

Suddenly, Dent hurled himself at the bin-bags, punching and kicking till they burst and their contents went flying. *'Garbage!'* he raged.

The two taller boys glanced sheepishly at the scattered rubbish.

'Someone should get round here with a brush and dustpan,' chuckled the one with a top-knot.

'Your mum!' sneered Dent. Noticing Lee, he scowled. 'What *you* looking at?'

Lee held out his hand.

Slapping Lee's palm, Dent walked off.

There was barely enough room to walk single file; Lee followed the others. The cut-through dropped down five steps, then widened suddenly into a large open space.

Dent pointed to the boy with the top-knot. 'That's Vinda,' he said, 'also known as *The Sikh Streak.*'

Lee nodded.

'And *that* is Leroy,' said Dent.

'Nobody calls me "Leroy",' said the black boy. He span the ball on his finger. 'Call me "Lee".'

'That might be difficult,' said Lee.

The three boys looked at him. '*Difficult?*'

'That's *my* name,' said Lee.

'How about nicknames?' said Dent.

'Never had one,' said Lee, praying his face wouldn't betray him.

'Well, what's your surname?' asked Dent.

Lee didn't blink. 'Mansfield,' he said.

'We could try calling him "Man" for short,' said Vinda. He chuckled. '. . . might be a bit confusing – *man on*, Man!'

'It's not going to work,' said Dent. 'Leroy, you're "Roy" from now on.'

'*Oi!*' The black boy sucked his teeth and scowled. '*Oi!*'

Vinda slapped him on the back. 'Very good! Now all you have to do is put an "R" in front of it – *Roy*!'

Lee turned his attention to the pitch.

The tarmac sparkled with broken glass; there were cracks and potholes, no lines or goal posts. The mesh fence sagged; litter lay in drifts.

'You get up early on a Sunday,' he said, 'to come and play on *this*?'

The three boys stared at him.

Dent's deep-set eyes narrowed to dark slits. 'We know it ain't Wembley,' he snapped.

'There's nowhere else,' said Vinda.

Grabbing the ball off Roy, Dent headed towards the far side of the pitch.

'What about broken glass?' Lee asked.

Roy laughed. 'Sliding tackles are *not* a good idea!'

Over by the fence, Dent placed the ball on the ground and tapped it back across the pitch. The ball made a series of little jerks and jumps as it travelled the rough surface. 'Great, eh?' he yelled.

Lee intercepted the zig-zagging ball.

'OK, hotshot,' yelled Dent, 'let's find out what you're really made of.'

Passing the ball, Lee sped off towards the far end. The pitch was hardly what he was used to, but then – what did he have to lose?

They were good – Lee was surprised . . . and *impressed*. Familiar with the unpredictable ground, Dent, Vinda and Roy took the ball off him again and again. They passed and received with precision. They chipped it, headed it, volleyed, chested it – keeping the ball in the air the whole time.

The tarmac was hopeless – rougher in parts than a gravel track; it was impossible not to trip. Roy went down first, cursing loudly. The knee of his jeans was ripped; his palm bled.

The pace slowed. They began to argue over favourite teams.

'See the footie last night?' yelled Dent. 'Brooksie?!'

Lee froze. Suddenly, he wanted to *vanish*.

'He should be in panto!' chuckled Vinda.

'He was funnier than Frank Bruno!' laughed Roy.

Lee prayed for something to happen, *anything* to change the subject.

'He was funnier than a footballer in flip-flops!' said Dent. He headed the ball across to Lee. 'What is that geezer *playing at*? If he don't pull himself together, he's finished.'

The ball was an awkward one. Shuffling backwards, Lee lost his balance. He tumbled.

Vinda chuckled; Roy and Dent laughed.

Lee checked his jeans – no rips, thank God! His palms were grazed, nothing more.

'Happens to the best of us!' said Dent.

Lee scrambled to his feet.

Suddenly, Dent snatched up the ball. 'Time to go!' he snapped.

'Hey?' Lee looked around. Roy and Vinda were already hurrying towards one of the larger gaps in the fence. 'I was just starting to enjoy myself!' he said.

'Your trial's over,' said Dent. He grabbed Lee's sleeve. 'You're on the team.'

Lee heard loud voices: harsh laughter, swearing and shouting – coming from the cut-through. 'Who's *that*?' he said.

'You don't want to find out,' said Dent. 'Now – *shift!*'

CHAPTER 5

Breakfast

Lee quietly closed the front door. He could hear Mum and Tanya laughing; the bedroom door was wide open. He peeped inside.

'The hero returns!' called out Mum.

'From his *recce*,' added Tanya, sniggering.

Propped up on pillows, they were snuggled together beneath the duvet. He was in for a teasing; two against one.

'Discover anything interesting?' asked Mum. There was a big smile on her face. 'How's the new life, *without football*?'

Lee sat at the end of the bed. 'OK,' he groaned, 'so I kicked a ball! I met these three boys from the estate.'

'How was it?' said Mum.

'They lark about a lot . . .'

'Surely not!' Mum feigned shock.

'Well – two of them do,' said Lee. 'Vinda and Roy. But the funniest is Dent.' He chuckled. 'He takes himself so seriously . . .'

Mum and Tanya nudged each other and smirked.

Lee scowled. What was so funny about that? 'They've got excellent ball skills,' he said, 'but it's all kick-about stuff – no strategies, tactics or set-plays.'

Tanya yawned.

'Like father, like . . .' Mum hesitated.

Lee glowered.

'Mum . . .' Tanya giggled. '– the bottom lip!'

'Yes, darling . . .' Mum sighed. 'Sorry, Lee . . . you were saying – about the boys?'

He cleared his throat. 'Sometimes they play friendlies against nearby estates. Dent's captain, he's asked me to join the team.'

'Great!' said Mum. She looked at Tanya. 'Doesn't waste time, does he?'

'They must be desperate,' said Lee. 'I mean . . .'

'Don't put yourself down!' said Mum. 'You've had your problems on the pitch, but there've been reasons – *we* all know how good you are.'

'The kick-about was nothing special . . .' mumbled Lee, '. . . but it was nice—' he shrugged, '– not being . . .'

'Brooksie – son of Brooksie?' said Mum.

Lee nodded. It had been great, once – being the son of England's most famous, most popular player; it had given him courage and confidence on the pitch, he had felt . . . *invincible*. 'I told them my name was Mansfield.'

Tanya gasped. 'He *lied*!'

'No . . .' said Mum.

Lee smiled. How would Mum get out of this one?

Tanya waited.

Mum puffed out her cheeks. 'I told Lee to use Mummy's name whilst we stay here.'

'We're *incognito*,' said Lee.

'Thank you,' said Mum. 'Yes, we're incognito.' She tapped the end of her nose. 'Mum's the word, and Mum's is the name!'

'Mumsie's the name!' shrieked Tanya.

'Football is the game,' muttered Lee.

Lee and Tanya lay under Mum's duvet. There was a delicious smell: fresh toast, hot chocolate and coffee. Mum was busy in the kitchen. It was a one-off treat: breakfast in bed.

The letterbox rattled.

Mum appeared in the doorway, carrying a tray. She walked gracefully and tall, even with both hands full.

Staring at the newspapers tucked under her arm, Lee fidgeted uncomfortably.

Mum handed out the buttered toast and hot chocolate. Tanya began to slurp and munch.

Lee's stomach was lead.

Mum frowned. 'OK,' she said, laying the papers on their fronts, 'let's get this over with.'

Lee watched her for a reaction. He wanted to lean over Tanya and take a look . . . but he couldn't move. Clutching his plate and mug, he waited.

'No pictures of you . . .' said Mum. Lee breathed. 'None of me, either.' She echoed his sigh. 'But I'm afraid there are three pictures of your dad – one in the *Observer* and two in the *Sunday Mirror* . . .' She shook her head. '. . . Dad, it seems, spent the match on his *derrière*.'

Tanya coughed particles of toast and marmalade as she dragged the newspapers in front of Lee. She started to giggle.

Lee glowered. Where was the joke? Three pictures of Dad – sprawled on his back, legs and arms in the air – waving goodbye to any last shred of dignity.

'Daddy's funny,' giggled Tanya.

'But only one person's laughing,' he snapped.

'Your breakfast, Lee,' said Mum, '– it's getting cold.'

He felt sick. 'BROOKSIE DOWN AND FINALLY OUT?' said one headline. 'BROOKSIE – SAD DECLINE OF BRIGHTEST STAR' said another. There was a smaller column with the heading: 'SUMMER REST & TRAINING – BROOKSIE'S LAST CHANCE OF REPRIEVE.'

'Lee?' said Mum.

He bit his lip.

'Dramatic pictures sell papers . . . they can be very cruel. Who knows? Your dad might have displayed some of his old form . . . the reporters are only interested in his slip-ups.'

Lee snatched up the paper. '"*People clearly felt cheated by Brooksie's abysmal performance*",' he read. '"*His walk from the pitch was greeted with jeers and boos . . .*"' He dropped back against the pillows. 'I hate him!'

44

They finished breakfast in silence.

Lee sipped miserably from his mug. Tanya's tiny fingers dabbed at crumbs; she eyed the abandoned toast on his plate. His outburst had ruined everything.

'I think we'd better have Sunday dinner *late*,' said Mum. She nudged Tanya. 'What you and I need now is some exercise.'

Suddenly, Lee remembered! He sat up and checked his watch.

'What's the matter?' said Mum.

'It's eleven-thirty!'

Mum and Tanya looked puzzled.

'Dent, Vinda, Roy—' said Lee, '– they want me to play . . . this morning over on the next estate. They said they'd call round – twelve o'clock kick-off!'

'Brilliant!' said Mum. 'Tanya and I can kill two birds . . .'

Lee put his hands together in a gesture of prayer.

Mum pouted girlishly. 'What?' she said in a hushed little voice, 'you don't want mummikins and sissikins to come along and cheer?' She and Tanya looked sorrowfully at each other. 'OK den,' whimpered Mum, 'I guess we'll go walkies somewhere else.'

Lee breathed a sigh of relief.

CHAPTER 6

'Local Friendly'

'Grovesnor FOUR! Sunningdale NIL!'

For a 'local friendly' the noise was deafening.

'We're being massacred!' yelled Lee.

'Get used to it . . .' grunted Dent.

Sunningdale were exhausted; they'd stopped chasing some time ago, but the half-time whistle still hadn't been blown.

Grovesnor's pitch was full-size Astroturf. They had the full eleven players; they looked like the junior Dutch squad in their orange and white strip.

Only nine had turned up to play for Sunningdale. The team had no kit; two of the players – a midfielder and the goalie – were playing in jeans!

Lee had never played for such a rag-bag side and never had to do so much running. The amazing thing was: in spite of the chaotic play and exhausting pace, he still had energy to run! He felt light on his feet, lighter than he had felt for months. For what it was worth . . .

'Mark up!' yelled Dent.

Lee glanced round. From the start, Grovesnor had been making the most of their two-man advantage; they were playing a numbers game – Sunningdale's penalty area was packed with orange shirts. Another assault was under way.

But you had to *try*. Lee checked his watch – less than three minutes to half-time. Might as well give it *everything*. He charged the oncoming forward, head-on. That ball was *his*.

'Go on, Lee!'

Yes!

Gottit!

'Nice one!'

His heart pounded. A goal before the whistle would give them something . . .

'I'm with you, mate!' Roy's yell came from the right. 'Let's *use* it.'

Orange shirts swooped from all sides. Lee sprinted. Let *them* do the chasing for a change. He swerved left . . . right . . . left . . . cutting sharply across the pitch, away from Roy. He jumped a scything tackle. A space opened up. He accelerated into it.

Shocked to see a Sunningdale player in their half with the ball, Grovesnor's midfield were slow to respond. Sensing danger, their supporters began frenziedly whistling and yelling.

Lee hurtled towards the goal. Ahead of him, frantic defenders barked instructions at each other. Flicking the ball to Roy, Lee kept right on, charging. He was well in amongst them before they realized their mistake. Roy was cutting round the flank.

'The wing!' yelled the keeper. 'Watch for the one–two!'

Defenders span for Roy, but *too late!* – the return pass was already over their heads.

Starting to come out, the keeper had a change of heart; he fell back and crouched low. The ball was dropping. Lee stretched his stride the last few steps – it would have to be on the left foot. Leaning to the right, he hooked the ball with the full force of the through-sweep – perfect!

'*GOAL!*'

*　　*　　*

'Keeper didn't have a chance, mate!'

'Nice one!'

Dent waited for the praise to finish before coming over. 'Left foot . . .' he nodded. '. . . *clever.*'

'Thanks,' said Lee.

'Beautifully set up,' said Roy.

'*Beautifully*,' sneered Dent.

They sat down, propped against the mesh fence; a giant bottle of cola was passed round. Behind them, supporters from the Grovesnor estate chatted and joked.

'Four–one!' exclaimed one. 'Must be Sunningdale's best ever half-time score.'

Dent grunted.

'Hang on to that scoreline,' chuckled another voice, 'and you'll be doing yourselves proud.'

There was laughter.

'Yeah – we're after double figures,' someone yelled.

'A *cricket score!*' yelled another.

Dent fumed.

'They're exaggerating,' said Vinda.

'Not much,' said Roy.

'You don't fancy your chances in the Sunday Afternoon League, then?' The man's voice came from behind the mesh.

'Very funny,' said Dent.

'I'm *serious*,' said the man. 'SAL's announced they're making an extra place in each division.'

Lee turned round. 'Yeah?'

The man's face was friendly. He nodded. 'There's so many new teams wanting to play in a league . . .'

'How are they choosing?' said Lee.

'Play-offs in each category,' said the man. 'Grovesnor have entered for the under-fourteens.'

'Great chance we stand, then!' snorted Dent.

Lee twisted. 'We should go for it!' he said. 'We've nothing to lose.'

'Oi!' Dent jumped to his feet. 'Who's captain here?!' He stood over Lee, glaring.

Lee shrugged. 'You, of course . . .'

'That's right!' snapped Dent. 'And don't you forget it!' He scowled and stormed off.

Scrambling to his feet, Lee followed after. 'A good captain listens to his team . . .' he muttered, coming up behind.

Dent showed no signs of hearing.

'Try Roy in goal,' said Lee.

Dent span round. 'Are you *barmy*?!'

Lee looked round. The others were watching. 'You're the boss,' he said.

Grovesnor were on their feet, limbering up for the second half. Sunningdale hadn't even thought about it.

'We've been playing like headless chickens,' said Lee.

'With nine men,' grunted Dent, '– what d'you expect?'

'We need to play more *tactically*,' said Lee.

Dent scowled. 'Our new manager!'

Vinda chuckled; Roy laughed.

'Listen—' said Dent, 'this isn't the Premier division – I'm lucky if I get the same players two games running.'

Vinda nodded. 'I've never even seen today's keeper before.'

'I never want to see him again,' groaned Roy.

Dent glowered at Lee. 'This is your first game,' he said. 'Sunningdale are *nobody*.'

Lee shrugged.

Dent turned to the rest of the team. 'On yer feet!' he yelled.

Shaking off their stiffness, the team gathered round. 'This half . . .' grunted Dent, '. . . stick to positions.' The team nodded sheepishly. Dent frowned. 'Roy . . .'

'Yes, boss!' chirped Roy.

' . . . In goal.'

'Sorry?' Roy stared as if Dent had spoken Greek.

'You heard,' said Dent.

'No way!' shrieked Roy. 'Look!' he slapped his thighs. 'Long legs – *runners* have long legs! Me, in goal . . .?' He tapped his temple. 'You're crazy!'

Dent drew himself up to his full height – a head shorter than Roy. 'I'm captain . . .' he snapped, '. . . you're keeper.'

The original keeper switched to left-back in place of Lurch – who had legs to match Roy's and took his place on the wing. The rest of the team stayed put – Vinda and Dent up front and Lee trying to hold together the middle.

Outnumbered and outmanoeuvred, Sunningdale blocked and tackled for all they were worth, but the Grovesnor onslaught was relentless: again and again they got through for a shot at goal. Roy leapt and dived, punched and grasped, grunted and swore. And the ball stayed out.

Sunningdale's forwards kept to their positions, waiting. Finally, there was a break. A defender pushed the ball through to Lee. He tapped it straight to Vinda, and they were off.

'*Yes!*' yelled Dent. 'Our turn!'

Sunningdale's midfield and forwards charged up the pitch. Frantically retreating, Grovesnor's midfield collided with their too-far-forward defenders.

Vinda passed to Dent. Lee followed in Dent's wake, charging past one orange shirt after another. Dent twisted, doubled back, twisted again, but the Grovesnor wolf-pack was gathering, his escape routes closing.

'Dent!' Lee pushed his way through the orange shirts.

Dent swivelled on the ball, glancing at Lee.

Lee signalled.

Dent grinned; he ducked, twisted and barged past two defenders.

All Lee could do was follow.

On the left, Vinda flapped his arms. 'Give it up!' he yelled. 'Come on, man . . . *pass* it!'

Surrounded and losing momentum, Dent suddenly stopped dead and back-heeled the ball.

It came straight to Lee. Dent was down, Lurch running in from the right and Vinda on the left. The home crowd yelled and hooted; they clung to the mesh fence, shaking their fists and spitting ugly threats.

Lee entered the penalty area with only the barest line on goal, between keeper and defenders. He kept his head: passed – neat and low – to Lurch, then ran hard for the post.

From the left, Vinda was racing in too. The goalkeeper yelled; defenders scurried to tackle Lurch. Waiting till the last moment, Lurch put it over their heads. Vinda, Lee and the keeper leapt together.

'Mine!' shrieked Vinda.

'Yours!' yelled Lee.

The goalie swung with his fist. The ball hit the back of the net. The lights went out.

CHAPTER 7

Tyler

The doctor had said Lee was fine; there had been a little light concussion, he should rest and take it easy. But that didn't make the slightest difference to Mum; he needed rest – he was grounded, indefinitely.

Gazing from the window, Lee watched Dent, Vinda and Roy making their way along the walkway.

Tall Roy, his posture kinked to one side from a pulled muscle, *shuffled*. Dent, his twisted ankle swollen to twice normal size, *limped*. Vinda's right eye was a swollen black beauty.

Mum took one look at them and sent them on their way.

'Try coming back,' she yelled, 'when your appearance is less distressful!' She dubbed them 'the Motley Crew' and warned Lee about mixing with 'the wrong type'. The Sunningdale was a *rough* estate, she told him – she'd grown up not far from it, she knew its reputation. His friends would have to shape up.

Lee pleaded with her. He told her about Dent, and how stubborn he was about listening to advice. He told her about the SAL play-offs. The team was scarcely even that – a team. They didn't have a manager or a coach! To have a chance, they needed to get organized. They needed *support*.

Mum offered him a deal: if he agreed to confinement, she would make some inquiries about SAL and the play-offs. They shook on it.

Boy! – did confinement go slowly. Back home there had always been plenty to do. He'd had his own room, his own CD-player, his own TV and video, his own computer and, of course – the garden. Now, he had none of that.

Outside the weather changed; lukewarm haziness gave way to scorching skies. Tanya developed hay fever overnight and had to stay indoors to avoid the pollen. Unable to remain silent for more than ten seconds, she pursued Lee around the flat, angling for attention. When she didn't get it, she resorted to irritation. His confinement became unbearable.

The Motleys, as Lee had now also taken to calling them, returned. Every day Lee reminded Mum that the goalie's whack to his head had been an accident, that Sunningdale's injuries had in fact all been accidents and that there'd been no fighting at the match. Finally, nearly one full week after his accident, she gave him permission to leave the flat.

As he headed for the door, Mum grabbed his arm and handed him a letter.

'It's just arrived,' she said, 'read it.'

'Ms Mansfield, Secretary, Sunningdale Under-Fourteens.'

Lee chuckled. '"Secretary"?'

'Temporary,' said Mum. 'I thought I'd better make it sound official.'

He read on.

'Dear Ms Mansfield

'Thank you for your enquiry concerning the forthcoming Sunday Afternoon League play-offs. Please note that the play-offs may need to be scheduled for both Saturdays and Sundays to ensure that all necessary matches may be played prior to the commencement of the season. Teams wishing to take part must ensure their applications are received by twelve o'clock, midday 7th August. There is a non-refundable fee of £50.

'Yours sincerely,

Mr S.J. Thomson
SAL *Secretary, South-East Region.'*

That's just over a week away,' said Mum. 'You and your Motleys had better get cracking if you want to take part.'

It was slightly unnerving to see a smile on Dent's face.

'What's the difference,' Dent demanded, 'between Brooksie and a sack of King Edwards?'

Lee stared at the ground.

'A couple of stone,' said Dent, '. . . and the transfer fee!' He sniggered and panted like a hyena.

Roy and Vinda fell about.

Lee tried hard to appear amused.

Dent stared. 'You don't look well,' he said. 'Perhaps that bang on the head was worse than we thought.'

As they wandered the walkways, passing a ball back and forth, Lee explained the news about the Sunday Afternoon League. To his surprise, Dent listened, nodded and grunted approval. Roy and Vinda grew excited.

The boys laughed, joked and chatted about the glorious 4–2 defeat with those who had been there and some who had not. But each time Lee tried to bring the talk round to the practical matters of training and finding the money to register for SAL, no-one, it seemed, wanted to bother.

'Is it just me,' said Lee, finally, 'who's serious about these play-offs?'

'Course not!' Dent frowned.

'Then why aren't we on the pitch, practising?'

None of them would look at him.

'You've seen the state of it!' mumbled Roy.

'Maybe we could have a go at cleaning it up,' said Lee. 'Where else is there?'

Roy and Vinda shrugged. Dent scowled.

'The yards are too cluttered,' said Lee, 'and as for these poxy narrow walkways!' He belted the ball so hard it ricocheted back and forth between the walls.

The Motleys remained silent.

'Suit yourselves!' said Lee. Trapping the ball, he turned and took off at a run.

'Hey!' yelled Vinda, chasing after him. 'Where are you going?'

Lee put on a spurt. 'Guess!'

'You can't!'

'Why not?'

'*Stop!*' yelled Dent.

Lee had reached the end of the walkway. He looked back.

'We'll take you,' said Dent, 'but not that way . . .'

Dent led the way. They started in a dark stinking chamber, where giant dustbins collected rubbish from overhead chutes. From here, by climbing between a dustbin and the wall, they were able to squeeze through a narrow opening. Outside, they had to reach across to a ledge. It was less than a brick's width wide and inching their way along seemed to take for ever. At the far end, they scrambled up a sloping roof and dropped down the other side to crawl through drifts of rubbish.

Loud laughter followed the sound of breaking glass.

Crouching amongst plastic crates and old shopping trolleys, Lee and the Motleys peered through gaps in the fence, like jungle explorers observing a secret tribe. They were very close.

'There . . .' croaked Dent, in a low voice, '. . . with the scar on his cheek.'

A broad-shouldered youth in vest and jeans stood stomping on broken glass. He had cropped black hair and tattooed arms. When the destruction was complete, he flexed his muscles and bowed. His companions laughed and clapped. The youth lit a cigarette, crushed the empty packet in his fist and flung it, contemptuously, into the air.

'Tyler,' whispered Dent.

'Loves to break things,' said Roy.

'Especially *people*,' said Dent.

'A good reason,' said Lee, 'to stay away?'

Vinda nodded towards the steps. 'He's another.'

A sumo-sized youth with a blond pony-tail blocked the cut-through. Wiping away a ketchup moustache, he tilted back his head and shoved a mountainous burger into his mouth.

'He'll choke!' gasped Lee.

'We should be so lucky!' hissed Dent.

'If that doesn't put you off burgers,' whispered Vinda, 'nothing can!'

From across the pitch came a loud, deep grunt of satisfaction.

'That's Tubs,' said Roy. 'Tyler's second-in-command.'

'He sits on people,' said Vinda.

Ripping a metal rod from a broken gate, Tyler picked up a brick and made his way to the pitch's centre. He tested the tarmac with his boot till he found a spot he liked. Then, ramming the rod into the ground, he shook it, banged it deeper and threw his weight against it with a loud grunt. Tarmac exploded into the air.

'He's wrecking it!' gasped Lee. 'He's digging up the tarmac!'

'Clever boy!' sneered Dent.

Lee glanced. He couldn't help thinking Dent had a sneaking admiration for the destructive performance.

From behind Tubs, a blond-haired, black

youth emerged on to the steps. He had a can of spray-paint in each hand and headphones on his ears. Singing and nodding, he graffitied the wall. Lee had seen the tag all over the estate, spray-painted in different colour combinations. It said: 'Sky'.

'Don't be fooled by happy boy,' said Roy, 'he's not always so peaceful.'

'He customizes cars,' said Dent, his mouth twisting into a smile.

'For free,' added Roy.

'You don't even have to ask,' said Vinda. 'He did my uncle's brand new Volvo six months back. Uncle was *not* pleased.'

Tubs devoured more hamburgers; Tyler dug up more tarmac; Sky continued with his artwork. Finally, Tubs and Tyler sauntered to the far end of the pitch.

Lee watched in silence as they began a kick-about.

Tubs moved surprisingly nimbly for such a large bulk, Tyler countered with strength and aggression. It was more like wrestling than football. The two of them pushed and shoved, hacked and kicked; scuffling their way up the pitch.

Lee watched his mates press themselves lower into the litter, as the two youths approached the fence. Suddenly, their frantic activity stopped. Tyler spat and bent over.

Lee could hear his pulse thrump in his ears.

'The tail's come off!' grunted Tyler. He straightened up. In one hand he held something long, thin and black like a stick of liquorice, in the other – something furry and . . . *matted with blood* . . .

Lee clamped a hand tight across his mouth. It was a *rat*!

Someone gasped.

Tyler span round, his eyes glared.

Lee's heart jackhammered against his ribs.

Tyler, grunting like some crazed animal, leapt at the fence.

Lee tried to shrink lower.

Tyler shook the fence and snarled ferociously. '*Intruders!*' he roared, and began to climb.

Tubs pressed his huge bulk up against the fence, his piggy green eyes piercing the shadows.

Sky charged across the tarmac, whirling

Tyler's metal rod above his head.

Lee glanced up.

Above them, Tyler shook his fist. 'Vermin!' he hissed, sniffing the air, like a dog. 'I recognize that smell . . . it's those *dribblers* . . .' He spat in disgust. 'It's those ball-kicking *brats*.'

Slashing at the wire mesh with the rod, Sky twisted back and launched it up over the fence.

As Lee looked up, it whacked against the wall above with a heavy clang, then fell clattering over his head and hit a shopping trolley.

'Time to scarper!' hissed Dent.

'This is stupid,' gasped Lee.

Vinda and Roy panted. Dent stared.

'Couldn't we discuss it on the move?' said Vinda. He nodded towards the road. 'I'd feel safer a little further away.'

After they'd jogged for a few minutes, with no sign of pursuit, Lee slowed up and began again. 'You've all gone on about getting a proper team together – how good it would be to train, get organized and maybe even get a coach . . .'

The three boys stopped and stared.

'The play-offs are a golden opportunity,' said Lee. 'Sunningdale won't get a chance like this for yonks. But without a pitch and the fifty-quid registration fee, it's never going to happen.'

'The pitch is Tyler's territory,' said Dent. 'End of story.'

'And no great loss,' said Vinda. 'You know how lethal that surface is.'

'As for fifty quid . . .' Dent turned and spat. '. . . where are we going to find that sort of dosh?'

Lee sighed. He knew it was true. Broken glass could be swept up, but the tarmac needed *serious* fixing. It would take ages and cost a fortune and they hadn't even the money for the registration fee.

'If you want me playing in goal,' said Roy, 'we need a softer surface to practise on.' He lifted his T-shirt; there were bruises up one side of his ribs. 'That's just from Grovesnor's Astroturf!'

'We need grass,' said Lee. 'What about nearby parks?'

Dent and his two side-kicks frowned as if he'd asked about local igloos, or sulphur pits.

'They don't go in for parks much round here,' said Vinda. 'The nearest is Burgess.'

'Twenty minutes on the bus,' added Roy.

'Parks are for pansies,' sneered Dent.

'People must walk their dogs?' said Lee.

The Motleys shrugged.

'They use the field . . .' said Vinda.

'The *what*?' said Lee.

'That.' Dent pointed. 'Dog toilet and rubbish dump all in one.'

Lee stared. They were right at the back of the estate, a part he hadn't been to before. On the other side of the road was what looked like a huge overgrown *meadow*. There were gaps where paths had been trodden through the yellowing grass; old broken furniture and bulging black bin bags had been dumped in heaps at the edges.

'It used to be a playing field,' said Roy.

'That?' said Lee.

'It used to be used by local schools,' said Vinda, 'but the council closed it down.'

'And now,' said Dent, 'it's going to become . . . a shopping centre.'

CHAPTER 8

News

'I can't believe it!' said Mum. 'The pitch – a *rubbish tip*?' Her hair was wrapped in a lime-green towel and she was wearing her dressing-gown; she looked oddly . . . glamorous.

She pegged a pair of Tanya's jeans to the washing-line, strung from drain-pipe to drain-pipe along the walkway. 'That,' she said, 'is where I assumed you and your Motleys have been playing. I remember it from years ago; Cherelle took me there.' She nodded to the peg-bag and held out her hand. 'A rubbish tip?' she repeated.

'Well, almost,' said Lee. He handed her two more pegs. 'It's all overgrown. Thistles and weeds; old mattresses, sofas, fridges, cookers and stuff – there's lorry-loads of rubbish. You'd never believe it had once been turf.'

Mum shook her head in disbelief. 'So where do kids play footie round here?'

'They don't,' said Lee, 'that's the point.'

Mum's head appeared between the legs of a pair of jeans? 'The point?'

'My plan . . .'

'Oh, yes . . .' A wary note crept into her voice. '. . . your *plan*.' Her brow furrowed. She was going to try and discourage him. 'I'm delighted you're back into football . . .' she said. 'You seem more enthusiastic than you've been for months . . .'

He was too tense to shrug.

'. . . but I think you should take things a little more gradually . . .'

He scowled.

'. . . I don't want you to be disappointed . . .'

'Mum!' he blurted, 'we *have to* have some kind of pitch!'

'I assumed you had,' said Mum.

Suddenly, Lee noticed – Mum was pegging out his underpants! Hot with embarrassment, he glanced around the yard. On display to the whole block!

Mum smiled. 'There's more to life than

football. If the boys round here don't play, I'm sure they find other things to do.'

'Graffiti . . .' said Lee. 'Vandalism, drinking and smoking, taking drugs . . .'

'Not your new friends, I hope!'

'No. They want to go for the league, but they're so used to having nowhere to play . . .' He scowled and kicked a plastic bottle. 'You did say there'd be a pitch to play on . . .'

Mum shrugged, hands on hips. '. . . and didn't somebody say something about giving up football?'

'Huh!' Lee turned away, arms folded.

'You're getting worse than your sister . . .' said Mum. 'OK . . .' she sighed. 'Go on then – tell me more about this plan.'

At last! He'd been sifting ideas in his head all morning – ideas for clearing the pitch, ideas for raising money – he had lots of them. He was desperate for an opinion.

As he opened his mouth to speak, a shuffling figure caught his eye. Bobbing along the walkway, head down, engrossed in reading something, it was . . . his dearly beloved sister. 'Tanya . . .' he groaned. He flopped back against the wall.

Tanya looked up. 'Hey!' she said, grinning from ear to ear, 'you're both famous!'

'What's this?' Mum almost *snatched* the paper from Tanya's hands.

'I found it,' said Tanya, 'on the stairs.'

Mum was frowning. Lee felt his blood drain away through the soles of his trainers. He clamped his bottom lip between his teeth. 'Famous' could only mean one thing.

The kettle was on.

Lee stared. A battered *News of The World* from the previous weekend. Two small fuzzy shots of him: one – wavy fringe and a hint of freckled nose as he twisted away; the other – legging it towards the pavilion, shirt over his head. There was a darker, fuzzier photo of Mum in sunglasses, head down and shielding her face to avoid the cameras.

'What does it mean?' said Tanya, wrinkling up her nose, '"Family Spilt"?'

'It means *you* can't read!' growled Lee. 'It says "Split", idiot, as in: coming apart.'

'*Lee!*' Mum glared. 'It says "Split", Tanya darling,' she explained, 'and it's all a load of nonsense.'

'*Brooksie's Shame – Family Split*?' Tanya tried the new meaning.

'*Marriage of thirteen years on the rocks?*' said the caption beneath Mum's photo. '*Wife and kids go into hiding*.' Beneath the two pictures of Lee it said: '*Like father like son?*' and '*What does future hold for Brooksie's boy?*'

'Brilliant!' snapped Lee. 'Just when we'd started to get settled . . .' He kicked the table.

Mum shot him a furious look.

'But I don't like it here!' blurted Tanya. Her voice wobbled. 'I *hate* it!'

'Now – *hey!*' said Mum, '. . . let's not start being miserable.'

Tanya's big brown eyes were suddenly full of sadness; she sniffed and rubbed her nose. 'Are you and Daddy getting divorced?' she said.

'No, darling, we are not!' said Mum. 'Newspapers will make a drama out of anything.' She emptied the boiling kettle into the teapot. 'It's just as I explained; we're staying here, so Daddy can have some time alone for a while . . . to sort out his little problems.'

Considering this statement for a moment, Tanya pushed up her eyebrows in a miniature copy of her mother's frown. 'What *are* his little problems?' she asked.

'Where have you been!' exclaimed Lee, scornfully.

'*Lee!*' snapped Mum.

'Dad is *fat*!' blurted Lee. 'He gambles all our money away. He eats too much, he *drinks* too much and he doesn't bother to train properly.'

'That's not true!' said Tanya. 'Daddy is *not* fat.'

'He's put on a bit of weight,' said Mum, wiping the worktop furiously, 'but I'd hardly describe him as *fat* . . .' She poured the tea. '. . . *Overweight* maybe.'

'He's *cuddly*,' said Tanya.

'Call him what you like,' said Lee, 'the point is, he's a *has-been*. Tomorrow, England play a team who've less than two years' experience at international level – and Dad can't even get himself selected!'

Mum and Tanya stared.

Lee couldn't stop. 'The few times Dad's played for the club this season, he's fallen over the ball more times than he's kicked it. If the club can find anyone to buy him over the summer, they'll sell. Everyone knows the knee's better.' His voice quivered with rage. 'Dad's given up – he just can't be bothered and everyone knows it . . .' Lee glowered '. . . except in this house.'

Silence.

His words hung in the air. He felt ashamed. He felt like crying.

There were tears in Tanya's eyes; she looked anxiously across to Mum and back to Lee again.

Mum carried the teas over to the table. Lifting Tanya on to her knee, she hugged her. 'It's particularly hard for Lee,' she said, bouncing Tanya like a baby. 'He's reached that age when boys can be a little impatient, a little inconsiderate, and sometimes – even a little *selfish*. To him, it matters dreadfully what *other* people think . . .'

Lee stared into his mug.

'. . . and particularly what they say and write about his dad because, as Brooksie's football-crazy son, *he* more than anyone feels the glory of Dad's success and the shame of his failure.'

Lee squirmed.

'Daddy isn't a failure,' said Tanya.

'No, I know, darling – of course not!' said Mum. 'He's been a bit down in the dumps . . .'

'Because he hurt his knee,' said Tanya.

74

'Yes,' said Mum, 'and it's taken a long while to get better . . .'

Her stare challenged Lee to say otherwise. He wanted to. He wanted to say: *That's not the problem – you know Dad's let himself go, he's lost the will, he's given up . . .*

'I spoke to Daddy on the phone earlier,' said Mum.

Lee stared.

Tanya jumped up excitedly.

'He's coming over to meet us tomorrow afternoon.'

What!? Lee's head span. 'Dad?' he blurted. 'Dad can't come *here*!'

'Yes, he can!' snapped Tanya.

'He *can't!*' Lee whacked the table with his fist.

'*Lee!*' Mum's eyes blazed.

'But, Mum!' Lee jumped up from his seat. '*This* is bad enough!' he yelled, snatching the newspaper and scrunching it furiously into a ball. 'If Dad comes here . . . we're finished!' He hurled the paper ball into the bin.

'*LEE!*' yelled Mum.

He gripped the back of the chair, shaking.

'*Stop* getting yourself all worked up.'

Mum's voice was steady but firm. 'Daddy isn't coming here.' She pulled Tanya towards her. 'He isn't coming to the estate,' she gave her a little kiss on the forehead, 'but he is coming over to this side of London. We're meeting him.'

'Will you be talking to him again before tomorrow?' said Lee.

'I said I'd call him to confirm, yes – why?'

'I need him to bring something . . .'

'If you want to tell me what it is, I can ask him for you.'

'My England football.'

CHAPTER 9

Dad

'If you make a scene,' said Mum, 'you'll attract attention.' She grabbed Lee's arm. 'We don't want that, do we?'

Of course he didn't! He didn't want any of it – didn't want to be treated like a kid, didn't want to be here, didn't want to see Dad, didn't want to hear what Dad had to say. He had things to be getting on with, important things – his plans for the pitch.

All happy to be dressed up, Tanya skipped ahead in her patterned dress. 'Daddy!' she squealed.

Sunglasses, light baggy jacket, baseball cap and several days' stubble. His disguise. Dad was always in disguise these days.

'Say hello to your dad, Lee.'

'Hello.'

'Hi-ya, kids!' The enthusiasm, the croaky voice and shadowy, bloodshot eyes blinking above the Ray-Bans were a dead giveaway.

Tanya squealed again and puckered up.

Lee shut his eyes and allowed himself to be kissed. Aftershave and extra-strong mints. Nothing masked the smell of booze.

Dad and Mum leant and kissed above him. Mum smiled, but there was sadness in her eyes.

Tanya, over-excited, jabbered and hopped flat-footedly. Dad coughed, trying to clear away some roughness. 'Well,' he said, 'can I get you all something to drink? They do nice cakes here too.'

'Chocolate, please!' piped Tanya.

Lee scanned his fingernails, selecting one to chew.

'Lee?' prompted Mum.

'Nothing.'

'*Lee!*' Mum scowled.

'Nothing,' repeated Lee, '*thank you.*'

Dad looked embarrassed. 'Louise?' he said.

'Coffee, please,' replied Mum.

*   *   *

78

'The Lyndhurst final got postponed?' said Dad.

'I walked off in the second half,' said Lee. When had Dad last come to see him play? When had Dad last asked about what he was doing, or how he was getting on? Not for a year. Lee shrugged. 'They're entitled to claim the game as theirs.'

'That would be unsportsmanlike,' said Dad.

Shot at goal. 'Talking of which . . .' said Lee, '. . . heard you played the last game of the season on your bum.'

Tanya tittered.

'*Lee!*' snapped Mum.

'No, Louise—' Dad was smiling. 'That's funny!'

Wide open goal – whack it home . . . Lee wanted to look Dad coldly in the eye, but he couldn't. 'You think so?' he said.

The cakes and coffees had arrived.

Mum stirred in her two sugars. 'Lee played a game last Sunday for the estate,' she said, 'against a neighbouring estate. They lost, but Lee says it was a good match.'

'Yeah?' said Dad. He leant across the table. The interested father.

Lee sank lower in his seat and stared at his fingernails.

Dad persisted. 'Didn't take you long to get involved, eh? How d'you get on?'

'I wasn't all that . . .' muttered Lee.

Mum patted his arm. 'The other boys were very impressed . . .'

Lee glowered. 'Some of them, maybe.'

'*All* of them,' Mum countered, her brown eyes brimming with pride. 'Some were just less vocal about it.'

'And what about them?' said Dad.

'They've got some real talent, but it's *raw* . . .'

'With a bit of nurture – eh?' Dad winked, clumsily. 'Get 'em practising, you know the drills . . .' He paused to cram gâteau into his mouth.

Lee forced himself to watch.

'Exceptional play . . .' Dad spluttered, 'is always a result of talent *and* practice.'

Wide open again. 'Yeah.' said Lee. '*We*, unfortunately, have nowhere to practise.'

Dad wiped his mouth.

'Lee's got this plan . . .' said Mum, trying to diffuse the tension. 'The local playing field has been allowed to go to seed. The council want to sell it off to developers . . .'

'And Lee's going to stop them? That's my

80

boy!' he chuckled, reaching out, to pat Lee on the head.

Don't you dare! Lee glared.

Dad thought better of it and withdrew the hand. 'What's the plan?'

'I'm working on it,' Lee muttered. Dad wasn't interested . . . didn't care less . . . and was certainly not going to offer him help or money.

Lee clenched his fists beneath the table. He felt like he'd snap. Dad had probably drunk and gambled every last penny anyway.

'A person can achieve anything,' said Dad, dropping two sugars into his coffee, 'they just have to set their mind to it.'

Open goal. Shoot.

Lee sneered. 'So what's stopping *you*?'

Dad didn't laugh this time. He stirred his coffee, and kept on stirring it.

Not even Mum seemed able to think of anything that might break the silent tension.

Suddenly, Dad bent below the table.

Lee felt himself grow hot, remembering his request.

'I almost forgot . . .' said Dad. 'Your England ball.'

Lee stared. His birthday present from

Dad, four years ago. Signed by every player of the England World Cup squad, Dad included. There were only a few like it; it was worth a lot of money – easily the most valuable thing he owned. It had always been the thing he most cherished – was most proud of . . .

'I know it's always meant a lot to you,' said Dad. 'Wanted to keep it near you, did you?'

Wide-open goal.

Shoot. What are you waiting for?

Lee reached forward and took the ball.

Dad grinned sloppily.

'I'm flogging it,' said Lee.

'You *what*?!' Dad coughed, spluttering coffee.

'I'm *selling* it.'

Tanya had demolished her slab of chocolate cake and drained her milkshake

Dad had regained his composure. 'I promised to take you two round a museum,' he said, 'then out for a pizza. Mummy has shopping and other jobs to do.'

Lee glared across at Mum – she hadn't mentioned this!

Mum cleared her throat. 'Actually,' she

said, 'I could probably use some help with the bags.'

'I'll go with Mum,' said Lee, swiftly.

Dad nodded.

Lee sat with Mum at a wooden picnic table on a patch of grass, beside an enormous car park. It was sunny. They were eating Sainsbury's sandwiches and drinking freshly squeezed orange juice.

His mood brightened. It wasn't often he got to spend time alone with Mum. It was even rarer for the two of them to be out together – even if it was only Sainsbury's.

'I know that stuff about selling your ball was just for reaction . . .' said Mum.

Lee shook his head.

'Don't be ridiculous!' said Mum. 'You love that ball!'

'We have to find fifty pounds for the registration fee,' said Lee, 'and that's just for starters. We have to have kit, and somewhere to play and practise . . . If we want to do this, all of us in the team are going to have to make sacrifices!'

'And you propose to sell your priceless ball?' said Mum. 'I'm not even going to argue with you – just make sure it's put somewhere safe when you get home.'

Lee grinned.

'What?' Mum frowned and dabbed at her mouth with a tissue. '*What?*'

Lee chuckled. 'You said *home*.'

'Well, you know what I mean.' Mum peered into his eyes. 'Is that how you're starting to think of it . . .?' she said. 'As home?'

Lee shrugged. 'I know we're not there for long . . .'

'But it's made a difference,' said Mum, 'hasn't it – being able to be plain old Lee, again?'

Lee nodded. 'The game last weekend – it was great; my concentration was back and I played . . . well – it's not saying much, but – better than I have all year. When will we have to leave?'

'Cherelle comes back the second week in September,' said Mum. 'The new football season will be well under way by then. But if Dad's still not fit – if he's been dropped, transferred or . . . *whatever*, then – who knows? We might have to make other arrangements.'

She put down her sandwich. 'Lee, I know it's not been easy . . . I know you, in particular, feel let down but . . .' she reached for his hand, '... don't you think you're being a little hard on Dad?'

Was he? In the café he had wanted to scream, he had wanted to break things, he had wanted to grab Dad and . . . *shake* some life, some sparkle, some *sense* into him. Dad's eyes were dead – switched off – the light had been missing for months. Behind the baseball cap and sunglasses – just an empty shell; the real Dad had gone. They'd been living with a stranger for the last year. Why should he be friendly to this stranger, this zombie? 'No!' he said bitterly. 'I want things like before. I want him back.'

'We all do,' said Mum.

There was sadness behind her smile – *that* was Dad's doing. 'I want you to be happy,' said Lee. 'I want us all to be happy . . .' He stared at his half-eaten sandwich. 'I want to be able to tell people my *real* name,' he said. 'When someone calls me "Brooksie", I don't want to feel ashamed.'

Mum squeezed his hand. 'Darling,' she said, 'you've got to be patient.' Her hands were elegant, but strong. She crossed his index and middle finger. 'With a bit of luck,' she said, 'by the start of the new season, things will have started to sort themselves out by then.'

'They won't!' he snapped, pulling away his hand.

'You're so sure?'

'It's not *things* that have to sort themselves out,' said Lee. '*Dad* does. Big time.' He clenched his fists. 'If he rings, or you talk to him, I don't want to hear about it! I just want to *forget* about him – *I don't want to know.*'

'It was really scary,' said Tanya, her voice shaky and vulnerable, 'they had painted faces . . .'

'White with a red cross?' said Lee.

Tanya nodded.

'England supporters,' said Lee, 'on their way home from Wembley.'

'I *know* that!' said Tanya. 'They were singing horrible rhymes about Daddy, outside the restaurant.' She dropped her head. 'And when we left, they ran after us, calling him names. People were staring.'

Lee chewed his lip.

'What sort of things were they shouting?' said Mum.

'I think . . . I'm not sure . . .' Tanya

fidgeted maddeningly, as she struggled to recall. ' . . . Stuff about his *figure* . . .'

Mum put a hand to her mouth; laugh lines showed around her eyes.

'And I think they said something about his *underwear*!' said Tanya.

'Hang on a minute!' said Mum, in mock outrage, 'that's a bit below the belt. There's nothing wrong with Daddy's underwear.'

'Daddy was really angry,' said Tanya, 'he started shouting . . .' She hesitated. 'He even *swore*.'

'Now, that *is* horrible,' said Mum. 'They must have been very rude young men – Daddy doesn't swear without good reason.'

Tanya's eyes widened. 'They were,' she said, '*very*.'

CHAPTER 10

Jackson

Lee, Dent, Vinda and Roy sat on a low wall, across the road from the field.

'Without a pitch – forget the league.' Lee slid from the wall and stood in front of them. 'You've got to have one – SAL's rules.'

Dent scowled.

Vinda and Roy stared at the overgrown site, their eyes trying to measure the effort that might be required.

'We'd need skips and JCBs,' said Vinda.

'Then combine-harvesters!' said Roy.

Lee nodded. 'We couldn't do it without equipment . . . and helpers.'

'There must be loads of others that'd join in,' said Vinda.

'There's naff all else to do round here,' said Roy.

'There's someone we should visit,' said Dent.

Dent rattled the letterbox. 'Jackson was the groundsman before the council closed the playing field.'

Beside the front door stood a wooden tub containing a small bushy tree. It was surrounded by assorted pretty pot plants – a splash of fragrance and colour, in Sunningdale's drabness.

'Heavily into the green stuff,' said Dent.

The door opened and an elderly man emerged. He was thin and bald. Squinting against the daylight, he examined the boys one by one; his gaze lingering finally on Dent. 'I know you . . .' he said, scratching his head and frowning, '. . . let me see . . . you're . . . you're the Denton boy!'

Dent nodded and turned to the others. 'Jackson and Dad are keen gardeners,' he said. 'Their allotments are next to each other. They've been friends for donkeys.'

Jackson nodded to Vinda and Roy. 'I've seen you two around the place,' he said.

Lee held out his hand. Jackson took it

and shook it with surprising vigour. There was a sparkle in his eye.

'Our latest signing!' said Dent. 'Lee's new to the estate.'

'Bit of a hotshot,' said Roy.

'Bit of a star,' said Vinda.

Lee shook his head, embarrassed.

Jackson stroked the small, neatly clipped tree at his side and grinned. 'Let's not beat about the *bush* – what's on your minds?'

'We want to go in for SAL's under-four-teens play-offs,' said Dent, 'we've got a footie team – but we've nowhere to play or practise.'

'And without a pitch you can't be in the league,' said Lee, 'so we're going to clear the old playing field.'

'Just like that?' Jackson chuckled.

'Dent thought you'd be the person to ask,' said Lee.

Jackson's smile widened. 'You'd better come in.'

The tiny living-room was cramped, more than half of it being given over to a dark wooden dining-table and chairs. An old television with buttons and knobs on, stood beside a glass cabinet. There were pictures on the walls and glossy pot-plants against the skirting.

The Motleys sat together on a collapsing old sofa. Lee crouched and peered at the collection of trophies and small framed photographs in the glass cabinet.

'This lemonade is flat,' whispered Roy. 'It's probably years out-of-date.'

Jackson appeared in the doorway, carrying two more glasses. He limped, but there was a sprightliness to his step. 'I don't often get visitors,' he said, handing Lee a drink.

'You played for Palace!' Lee nodded towards the cabinet.

'And the Gunners.' Jackson eased himself into the worn-looking armchair. 'Six years of professional soccer . . . all brought to an abrupt end . . .' He slapped his right leg. 'Knee cartilage.'

Lee shuddered.

The Motleys noticed.

'Horrible!' said Lee, trying to cover his reaction.

Dent nudged his companions. 'Bit squeamish, are we?'

Lee shrugged.

'If my injury had occurred today,' continued Jackson, 'they'd probably have had me up-and-running after a week.'

'Then you became a groundsman?' said Lee, keen to move on.

Jackson chuckled. 'Nothing could've been further from my mind. I was twenty when I turned professional, twenty-six when it ended in '55. I stayed in the game for thirty more years – as a coach.'

A coach! Lee could hardly believe his ears. Dent had said nothing about this – he looked as surprised as the others; he'd clearly had no idea.

If they could persuade Jackson to get involved . . .

Jackson's gaze was distant. 'But that's the past . . .' he muttered, shaking his head. 'Tell me, how can I help in the present?'

'Could we do it?' said Lee. 'Could we clear the pitch?'

Jackson took a sip of tea. 'Is there just you four?'

Lee nodded. 'So far.'

'Wrong!' said Dent sharply. 'Every team member helps, or they don't play.'

'Any funds?' said Jackson.

Lee shook his head. 'I reckoned we'd have to hire skips and bulldozers . . .'

Jackson nodded.

'. . . plus special mowers to cut down the high grass . . . we could have a big jumble sale—'

'– *or* a car boot sale,' interjected Dent.

'Yeah,' said Lee, 'to raise the money – and that would get people involved.'

'Even supposing you raise enough to hire all this equipment,' said Jackson, 'and you get the support you'll need from people on the estate, there's a good chance that after this much time the playing field won't be fit for donkey-riding, let alone soccer.'

Dent scowled. Vinda shook his head. Roy kissed his teeth. Their glances said: Lee had been wasting their time with his stupid idea.

'With the grass its current length,' said Jackson, 'if you cut it, you'll just be left with dry brown stems. There're mice, foxes, rabbits, rats and plenty else living there; the grass will be coarse, the ground may be worse.'

Lee chewed and twisted the remains of a fingernail.

'Then,' said Jackson, 'there's the small question of what you plan to do when the owners come along and kick you off!'

'It's owned by the council,' said Dent.

'It *was*,' said Jackson. 'Now – who

knows? The council have been trying to strike a deal since before they closed it down.'

'Wouldn't they make some kind of announcement if they'd sold it?' said Vinda.

'This lot?' A smile rippled across Jackson's cheeks. He shrugged. 'I doubt it – some of them's up to *all sorts*. Believe me, that playing field's not laid derelict for so long without reason.' Leaning forward, he put a finger to his lips. 'Conversations I overheard during my days as groundsman,' he said, 'suggested that a certain councillor is set to make a tidy sum when this shopping centre finally gets built.' His eyes widened. 'I shan't name names, but let's just say: someone *local*.'

'Tyler's dad!' said Dent.

Jackson smiled.

'In the meantime,' said Lee, 'the pitch goes to waste.'

'Sometimes these deals don't go quite as smoothly as intended . . .'

'All we need is grass,' said Lee, 'some white lines and two sets of goal posts.'

'Good job!' said Jackson. 'The council demolished the pavilion when they made me redundant.'

Lee glanced at the Motleys – they looked as downcast as he felt.

'Turf needs maintenance – mowers, rollers and the like. You'd need somewhere to store the stuff and someone to look after it all.' Jackson winked. 'I might be able to arrange something on that score. I might even know where we could get our hands on some of the equipment . . . but you'd have nowhere to change, nowhere to shower . . .'

'We don't need any of that!' said Lee.

'We don't need showers,' laughed Roy.

'And we've no kit to change into,' chuckled Vinda.

'All we need,' said Lee, 'is a pitch.'

'It'd be a mammoth task.' Jackson's eyes twinkled warmly. 'But if you want my help, I'll see what I can do.'

CHAPTER 11

Action

'Friday's the closing date for registration,' said Mum. 'Your first game's . . .'

'We're *registered*?' said Lee.

Mum nodded. 'Saturday's your first match.'

The four boys stared. '*Saturday!?!*'

'Yep,' said Mum. 'The league secretary was sympathetic; he's given you an *away* – so you'll have a bit more time to sort out your home pitch.'

Lee groaned. 'One week more . . .'

That gave them just *ten days* to come up with a pitch they could play a match on. Could the field be transformed in that time? Was there even a *remote* chance? It was ridiculous to try, wasn't it? They'd got their first match in three days' time – they didn't even have a full team! Preparing for that was going to take every minute they had. The pitch might be so damaged by years of neglect it couldn't even be used . . .

Mum handed him the letter. 'Your first opponents are a team called Charnley.'

The Motleys shook their heads – they didn't know the team.

'What about the registration fee?' said Vinda.

'You can pay me back when the money starts pouring in!' said Mum.

Lee grinned. He could've hugged her.

She leant and whispered in his ear. 'So now – no need to sell the football!'

'Thanks, Mum!'

'Thanks!' echoed Vinda and Roy. Dent shrugged and grunted.

'Now,' said Mum, 'when's your fund-raising day?'

'Sunday,' said Lee. 'We're making the leaflets and posters this afternoon.'

'You can tell people about the match as you deliver them,' said Mum. 'When it comes to clearing the pitch you'll need all the help you can muster – the more support you gather now, the better.'

*   *   *

Lee had never been particularly artistic or good with words, but he found himself taking charge of the leaflet. Dent, proclaiming himself 'completely allergic to writing and art', had refused to contribute so much as an opinion, let alone pick up a pen. Vinda and Roy spent most of the time acting the fool and squabbling about each other's suggestions.

The final design was simple, neat and clearly laid out. He had aimed for the snappiness of a newspaper headline. SUPPORT THE SUNNINGDALES it said in big bold capitals and RECLAIM THE TURF. The fête would include: car boot and jumble sales, a barbecue, a raffle, displays of football skills and various stalls and competitions.

At the bottom of the leaflet it said: ALL DONATIONS TO THE SUNNINGDALE PITCH CAMPAIGN GRATEFULLY RECEIVED.

Whilst Mum took the design to get copies printed, Tanya helped Lee, Vinda and Roy to make bright and colourful posters.

Lee and the Motleys met early, down in the yard. The morning was already hot.

Word was – Britain's summer had finally arrived.

'If we're organized,' said Lee as they began pushing leaflets through letter-boxes, 'we can do these, put up the posters and select the team all in one day. That'll give us one less job to worry about. We might even find time to train!'

Dent chuckled. 'Sure!'

Vinda and Roy shook their heads doubt-fully.

'So much for Sunningdale's fighting spirit!' muttered Lee.

Dent scowled.

The day grew hotter. Many front doors and windows were propped open to increase air circulation. Curtains were kept closed to shut out the sun.

Word was – this was the start of a *heat-wave*.

In the yards, ice-cream vans drew queues for lollies, cornets and cold drinks. Sunningdale's stifling flats were aban-doned for the cooler walkways and balconies. Everybody was sticky – from heat and sweetness.

With the news that the team were going for a position in the Sunday Afternoon League, now suddenly, anybody who had ever played with Dent wanted to be selected.

As Lee and his three mates trudged round the sweltering estate, Dent selected players for the team. Training began immediately on selection and consisted of joining in with the delivery of the leaflets!

Enthusiasm and excitement seemed to swell with the heat. Many of those not lucky enough to be picked for the first match were still full of hope and keenly offered to help with the fund-raising day and with clearing the pitch, as did brothers and sisters.

Mothers, once they learned about the jumble sale, rushed indoors to start sorting through cupboards and chests of drawers for old unwanted stuff that could be got rid of. Lee and the Motleys were offered items as prizes for the raffle – bottles of wine, a bottle of whiskey, a box of chocolates.

The estate seemed to go on and on for ever. Every time Lee thought the job was finished, another walkway would lead into another block or yard they hadn't visited. But by the time it was dark, they had delivered leaflets to every single flat on the estate – as he had said they could.

Exhausted, he fell asleep on the sofa, his dinner not even half-eaten.

*   *   *

'Come on!' yelled Jackson. ' I asked you all to be here at seven-fifteen a.m. – it's nearly half-past! We're wasting valuable training time.'

Vinda, Roy, Lurch . . . Junior and Jack – the two small midfielders . . . Grant, Thomas, Anton and Sean – the defenders: they were all there.

Lee tried to run. His body ached.

Dent grunted along, ten metres behind him.

The morning's training began.

First, a twenty-five minute jog round the estate. Then, a series of stamina and speed exercises – shuttle-runs back and forth between cars, press-ups, crunches and star-jumps.

Because of the yards' restricted space and the hardness of the ground, there was much they couldn't practise, but Jackson had them concentrating on ball control: heading, short passes, and dribbling skills – around markers between the cars.

When they took a break at ten o'clock, Lee was on his knees and gasping.

Jackson had kept them all working full tilt, in spite of the heat. He was a ruthless coach for such a quiet, smiling man. But then – Lee looked round at the flushed, panting and sweating faces of his team-mates – to get such a rabble into shape for Saturday, ruthlessness was needed.

After a lengthy stretching session, they retired to the shade for a discussion on systems and tactics, everyone worn out and grateful for the chance of rest.

Each day, after training, the team had more and more work to do. Mum was letting them use the front room of the flat as a depot for jumble. She had enlisted some of the volunteers to help her and Tanya sort it out.

Sometimes people delivered stuff, but more often they rang or left a note asking for it to be collected. It was the team's task to lug the bags of clothes up and down stairs and along the walkways.

On the Friday before the match, Lee went with Jackson and the rest of the team, by bus to Burgess Park.

'Grass at last!' he yelled, as they ran through the gates. It would be an opportunity to practise tackling and set-pieces, as well as shooting and passing over longer distances. And – for Roy – the chance to practise diving for the ball.

Jackson divided them into two small teams to try out the tactical ideas he had discussed during the week. Every ten minutes, he swapped players around, to get an idea of how everyone performed – individually and together.

On the bus home, Lee found himself *longing* for a hot foamy bath. He couldn't remember ever wanting one quite so much – and in the middle of such hot weather!

He looked around. There probably wasn't a single Sunningdale player who didn't feel the same way. Except perhaps Dent. If Dent had such longings, he would never admit it.

'*Charnley, cha-cha-cha! Charnley, cha-cha-cha! Charnley, cha-cha-cha!*' The chant easily penetrated the changing-room walls. Sunningdale were 2–0 down.

'If it's anyone's fault, it's mine.' Jackson handed round juice. 'I've overworked you these last few days.'

Lee scanned the faces. Everyone looked exhausted.

The afternoon was an absolute scorcher. They'd only played for thirty-five minutes – but it felt like full-time.

Roy walked into the changing room.

Lee gave a loud whistle. If it hadn't been for Roy, the score would have been a lot worse. And whose idea had it been to put Roy in goal?

The rest of the team cheered and clapped.

'Thanks for keeping me so busy,' said Roy, bowing. 'I needed the extra practise!' He pointed towards the door. 'Our supporters are outside – they've just arrived. A bus broke down, apparently.'

'Listen!' said Lee.

The team hushed. Behind the voices of the Charnley supporters, a chant of '*Sunningdale!*' could clearly be heard.

'They'll have some anger to vent,' said Jackson, 'because of missing the first half. They've got fresh voices and buckets of energy – they're going to go bananas when you walk back out there.'

The team grinned.

'Your confidence, lads, is about to *soar*.' Jackson looked from face to face. 'Two goals – what's that? With supporters cheering you on, you can score two goals in two minutes – no problem.'

'*Yeah!*'

'*Sunn-ing-dale! Sunn-ing-dale! One . . . more . . . GOAL!*'

Lee half-jogged half-floated back

towards the Sunningdale end. The supporters were *fantastic!* When he'd scored the first goal they'd gone wild. Now Dent had put away the equalizer. They were going totally *bananas* – just like Jackson had said!

Jackson was on the touchline, talking to a bearded man in a floppy sun hat. Next to them, Mum and Tanya held up their home-made banner and cheered with the others. On an old sheet, in huge letters was written: SUNNINGDALES. It looked like Tanya's colourful handiwork. Lee gave a little wave.

Charnley didn't look quite so sure of themselves: their shoulders in their maroon shirts had dropped, their heads hung lower. Their coach scowled and bellowed. On the pitch, their fiery copper-haired captain dashed about, barking commands at his flagging team. Their supporters waited glumly for something to cheer.

'Let's wipe 'em out!' yelled Dent, from up front.

Charnley started a cautious push, trying to keep the passes short.

Dent, Vinda and Lurch harried and attacked.

Passing back to hang on to possession, Charnley kept trying to turn it around, but they were losing ground all the time.

Lee spotted his moment. Charging hell-for-leather, he intercepted a pass and . . . took off with the ball across the pitch.

The supporters roared.

He snaked, like an out-of-control drag car; one after another, he dodged Charnley's attempted interceptions. Three strides from the penalty area came the inevitable clumsy tackle – high and late enough to chop his legs from under him. But anticipating it, he leapt clear.

'Nice one, Lee!' Dent was up with him, on the right.

Maroon shirts packed the penalty area. The only way a ball was getting through was if someone took it all the way.

Lee looked across: Dent was pushing on, down the middle; over on the far side, Lurch was streaking in from the wing.

'Lee!'

He twisted round. White shirt, shorts and top-knot, Vinda sped towards the near-side post.

Lee faked a pass. Maroons moved to intercept. He ran into the gap.

'Lee!'

Lurch, running in his peculiar head-jerking style, was ploughing like some crazy turbo ostrich *right towards him*.

Leaving him the ball, Lee took off towards the goal. It wasn't a set-piece, it wasn't a move they'd ever rehearsed, but it worked like a charm: Charnley players virtually fell over each other as, ball-less, he bobbed his way through.

He turned and called. Defenders bunched in tight round him, four of them trying to block him out.

Dancing with the ball, backwards towards the edge of the box, Lurch looked up and chipped the ball to Vinda.

Vinda volleyed it over the penalty area.

Half a dozen players leapt.

But Dent's head made the contact!

At the last minute, Lee saw the ball coming straight *at* him. He flung himself backwards, kicking up his legs. His left foot made contact. He felt it – an overhead volley.

And even upside down, he could see it – *hit the back of the net!*

The roar was deafening.

CHAPTER 12

Fête

Lee couldn't help feeling a touch of pride. Overnight, the winning goal had become a legend.

Touring the estate to remind people of the afternoon's fête, he and the Sunningdales were discovering they had become heroes. Everyone wanted to talk about the winning goal. Unfortunately, this was causing problems.

Dent reckoned the goal had been his.

Lee knew otherwise, but so far he had kept his mouth shut – *for what it was worth*. People on the estate seemed to be in no doubt that the goal belonged to him.

And as the team did their rounds, they were saying so.

There were storm-clouds in Dent's eyes; his face was thunderous.

'We're on the same side, aren't we?' said Lee, trying to find words that might pacify. 'What does it matter *who* scored?'

'It matters!' Dent snapped. 'Course it matters!'

'Not enough!' said Lee.

Sean, Jack and Junior – the boys standing closest – stepped back.

Dent stood in front of him, glaring.

'What matters,' said Lee, 'is making sure the fête goes smoothly . . .'

'Of course!' Dent scowled. 'Your little fête!'

'Ours!' snapped Lee. 'All of ours . . . our only chance to raise money and gather support . . .'

Dent glowered.

The group around them was growing larger. Heads bobbed.

'. . . it's the only chance we'll have to get ourselves a pitch . . .' said Lee, '. . . our only chance to go for the league. This afternoon is important, you *know* it!'

Dent was right up close. *In his face.*

'If I hadn't got my foot to that ball . . .' Lee hissed through clenched teeth, '. . . it was going to hit the post!'

'*Cobblers!*' Twisting away, Dent barged through the gathered crowd. 'Out of my *way*!' he yelled. 'Out of my WAY!'

Overseen by Jackson, a display of foot-balling skills by the Sunningdale squad started the afternoon's events in front of an enormous crowd. The whole estate seemed to have turned out – in shorts, sandals and T-shirts. They packed the central yard.

Then the selling began. Tables of jumble-sale clothes became a rush of fren-zied activity as people fought to discover bargains.

Down at the car boot section of the yard, things were a little more dignified and the objects for sale a little more varied. Stalls selling home-made beer and lemonade had sold out in the first hour and home-made cakes and cookies, generously baked and donated by local mums, were doing bril-liantly.

Working behind one of the jumble stalls with Vinda and Roy, Lee glanced at his watch. In thirty-five minutes, Mum was due to hand out prizes for the competitions and raffle. Then she was going to announce how much the afternoon had raised.

Following the display of football skills, Jackson had returned to his flat to make his final calculations of what clearing and repairing the pitch would cost. In thirty-five minutes, Sunningdale would know if they had a future . . . He had to talk to Jackson.

He tapped Vinda on the shoulder. 'Back in a minute . . .'

Vinda nodded.

Reaching for the bag by his feet, Lee slipped under the table and into the crowd.

The yard was jam-packed with people of all ages. There were many he recognized from delivering leaflets and picking up jumble, and plenty more he did not. Word about the fête had clearly spread beyond the estate.

Pushing his way through the crowd, he rehearsed what he was going to say.

'Lee!' Jackson waved from the walkway. 'Wait there, mate – I'm coming down.'

Lee found a space at the bottom of the stairwell, where it was less crowded.

'The whole estate's buzzing with excitement!' Jackson galloped down the stairs. 'I must have been stopped a dozen times – everyone wanting to talk about the team's success and hear about the famous goal.'

Lee smiled.

'It's certainly busy!' said Jackson, nodding towards the crowded yard. 'Looks like being quite a success!'

'I hope so,' said Lee. 'All the equipment and machinery we'll have to hire . . .'

'That's what I wanted to talk to you about . . .' Jackson's smile lines appeared. 'You remember I mentioned the mowers, rollers and other gear that used to be there in my days as groundsman?'

Lee nodded.

'Well, I'd grown rather attached to them over the years . . . so, when the council closed the place down and the whole lot was taken away to be turned to scrap, I had a little word with the contractor.' Jackson winked. 'We made an *arrangement*. He's been keeping 'em safe. So – we can get a good deal on *that* score.'

'Brilliant!' said Lee. Scoring goals – and now *this* – perhaps his luck was starting to change . . . 'It's skips and a JCB we've got to worry about, then?'

Jackson chuckled. 'This contractor bloke runs plant hire and skips, as well as scrap – he's going to sort us something out.'

'Wicked!'

Jackson wagged a warning finger. 'Don't go counting your chickens – there's plenty of other costs yet: long grass cutters for starters, seed and fertiliser, more than likely, to bring the pitch up to scratch . . .'

'Oh . . .'

'. . . Patches of turf will almost certainly have to be replaced – and that can get very costly.' Jackson shook his head. 'I've made my final estimate of what it all might come to . . . it's still a heck of a lot, I'm afraid!'

'That's what I wanted to talk to *you* about,' said Lee. He held out the bag.

'What's this?' Jackson shuffled the two carrier bags he was holding and looked inside Lee's.

'A ball,' said Lee. 'It's signed by the England World Cup squad. It's supposed to be worth quite a bit.'

Jackson rotated the ball through his fingers, reading the signatures.

'If we haven't raised enough,' said Lee, 'I want you to sell it.'

Jackson looked up from the ball.

'I thought – a kind of mini-auction?' said

Lee. 'After Mum's announcement? I don't want anyone to know it's mine.'

'Who gave you this?' said Jackson.

Lee swallowed and met Jackson's gaze. 'It *is* mine,' he said. 'Will you sell it?'

Jackson's eyes flickered back and forth, studying Lee's face.

'This must be the most precious thing . . .'

'The most *important* thing,' Lee interrupted, 'is that Sunningdale get a pitch.'

Jackson sighed and stroked his dome. 'I can see this is not a decision you've taken lightly . . . Well – I suppose, if your mother doesn't disapprove . . . there's no reason I shouldn't do what you ask.'

Lee shrugged. Mum knew about his plans to sell the ball, to raise the registration fee – she hadn't said he couldn't . . . She wouldn't be particularly happy, but she'd understand. She wouldn't *prevent* him.

'You can ask her,' he said. He turned towards the crowded yard. 'Anyway, with this much support – who knows? – we might not need it.'

'Not everyone supports the campaign,' said Jackson. He nodded at the wall beside him. One of the Sunningdale posters had been torn and defaced. 'I've seen several in the same state,' he continued, then he held up the ball. 'What's the minimum asking price?'

'Fifty . . .?' said Lee.

'I wouldn't let it go for less than double,' said Jackson. A sly smile crept across his lips. 'And I reckon you'll do a lot better than that.'

Lee pushed his way through the crowd. There was no mistaking the voice he'd just heard. Nor its tone . . .

'I said – *out of my way*, fatso!'

He hadn't seen Dent since the afternoon's skills display – Dent had turned up late, scowling heavier than ever, done the routine *superbly*, then vanished into the crowd.

The voice was rising louder and louder. '*Yes!* I called you *FATSO!*'

Suddenly, Lee caught sight of Dent – backed up against a wall and surrounded by the three thugs from the tarmac pitch: Tyler, Tubs and Sky.

Passers-by were giving them an extra-wide berth, but apart from that, took little notice.

Red in the face, Dent raged and tried repeatedly to get away from the wall. Every time he made a move, huge Tubs shoved him back.

Tyler twisted round. 'What's this – the dribblers' newest recruit?'

Lee froze.

'Well – the more the merrier!' said Tyler. 'We was just explaining to this little snotrag how we felt about your crummy pitch campaign . . .'

Lee stared.

Tyler tilted forward. A long, knotted string of saliva trailed from his mouth. It pulled its way slowly down on to the leaflet in Tyler's hand.

Sky did the same.

Tyler spat to release the phlegm. 'Your leaflet,' he said, 'is a load of *dribble!*'

Grabbing Dent, Tubs dragged him, kicking and struggling, towards Lee.

Sky gave a mad, high-pitched laugh, like a hyena.

Lee felt himself shaking. His stomach churned.

Tyler leant close. They were face to face.

Right in front of Lee's nose, once, twice, three times, Tyler tore the dribble-covered leaflet in half.

'Take my advice,' said Tyler, 'keep your nose clean . . .' Grabbing Dent, he pushed him at Lee. 'Stay away from *dribble*. Dribblers are losers!'

116

*   *   *

Standing with Mum and Tanya in the centre of the crowd, Lee tried to shrug off the feeling of fear.

He looked around: no sign of Tyler and his gang. Dent, Vinda and Roy were close by. Dent hadn't said a word.

Just in front of them, Jackson strutted back and forth on a table. 'Ladles and jelly-spoons . . .' he boomed, '. . . boils and curls!'

The crowd laughed.

Jackson held up his arms for hush. 'It's been a fantastic afternoon, but I'm afraid we're still a tad short of what I've esti-mated. Not all the money's been counted up yet, but it's clear we're going to need a little more . . .'

Jackson bent and rummaged at his feet.

Lee took a deep breath and sneaked a glance at Mum. She was smiling.

'So!' boomed Jackson, 'all you collectors of football memorabilia out there – of which I'm certain there are many – cheque books and pens at the ready! An impromptu auction – your chance for the bargain of a lifetime!'

Lee shut his eyes.

'*Ooooh!*' chorused the crowd.

'One complete Arsenal Football Club

strip from the year 1955 – before most of you were born, I shouldn't wonder!'

The crowd laughed.

Lee opened his eyes. Jackson was holding up a red and white shirt.

'. . . it's practically antique . . .'

The crowd laughed again.

'. . . this very strip worn by yours truly – washed since, of course . . . *and* . . .'

The crowd were loving his showmanship.

'. . . one genuine England World Cup medal!'

'*Ooooh!*' chorused the crowd again.

'What am I bid for these?' boomed Jackson.

The bidding started.

'Thirty pounds . . .'

'Fifty!'

'Seventy-five . . .'

'One hundred!'

The crowd held their breath.

'One fifty!'

'One seventy-five . . .'

Lee jerked round. Mum had thrust her hand in the air. 'I bid *three hundred pounds!*' she yelled.

'Glad to see we've got some serious collectors here this afternoon!' Jackson raised the shirt and medal above his

118

head. 'Anyone top three hundred?'

The crowd fell silent.

'Nobody going to top this fine bid?' Jackson scanned the yard. 'Going once . . . going twice . . .' Jackson stamped his foot on the table. '*Sold* to the lady at the front!'

Lee watched as the people in front moved aside so Mum could collect her purchases. His heart was trying to jump out of his chest.

Jackson straightened himself and cleared his throat.

The excited crowd hushed once more.

'The second and final item in this afternoon's auction is this unique football!'

He caught Mum's glance. His heart was beating so fast, it felt like it would *explode*.

'. . . from the last World Cup, signed by every member of the England squad . . . a rare and valuable item indeed . . . what am I bid?'

'Twenty-five pounds!'

'What! Sorry, sir – did I hear you say "*twenty*-five"?'

'All right then: *thirty*-five!'

'You're having me on!'

'Fifty!'

'Better!'

'One hundred.'

'That's more like it!'

'One fifty!'

'Two hundred!'

'Two twenty-five . . .'

'Two thirty-five . . .'

'Two fifty!'

Lee crossed his fingers.

Jackson scanned the crowd. 'Two-hundred-and-fifty-pounds – to the man in the suit. Am I bid any more?' Suddenly, he stopped and stared.

The crowd shuffled and murmured with excitement.

Lee held his breath.

'Ah yes, you, sir – is that a bid? It is? You're holding up your hand, sir – that's five fingers – do I take that to be a bid of *five* hundred pounds?!'

Lee stretched up on his toes and craned his neck, but everyone else was doing the same thing.

'Any advance on five hundred pounds?' yelled Jackson.

The crowd fell silent.

'Then *sold*!' yelled Jackson, 'to the man in the hat – for *five* hundred pounds!'

Jackson was already waiting when Lee and his mates arrived. Stood, with his back to the estate, gazing out across the over-grown pitch, he didn't turn to greet them.

The sun had sunk low. The horizon shimmered.

They stood beside Jackson in silence.

As the last sliver of sun slipped beneath the world, gentle breezes rippled the field like a golden sea. The field seemed to sigh.

'Almost seems a shame to cut it,' said Lee.

Hypnotised, the others stared and nodded.

'Still . . .' said Jackson, 'there's nothing quite as beautiful as a freshly mown football pitch, whatever the time of day!' He rustled in his pocket. 'Humbug anyone?'

The spell was broken. A bag was passed around; fingers fumbled with wrappers.

'In big cities,' said Jackson, 'people need open spaces, so they can grow.'

Dent made a scornful snorting noise. 'Vinda and Roy have done all right – considering!'

'Space . . .' said Jackson, 'is *priceless*. They should never be allowed to sell it off . . . or fill it in.'

Lee looked at his friends: Jackson – arms outstretched, Dent sneering, Vinda and Roy nodding and chewing. None of them knew him. None of them knew *Lee Brooks*.

They didn't know who he really was – know about the big house, the acres of garden and the full-size snooker table in a room to itself. *He* had always had space to play – till now. He had been lucky.

Selling the football had been the right thing to do.

CHAPTER 13

The Pitch

Lee woke with the dawn. Skipping breakfast, he slipped out before Mum or Tanya stirred.

The first stage of the clean-up operation was already under way when he reached the field. Shining in the seven o'clock sun, a bright yellow JCB manoeuvred along the edge of the overgrown field like some monstrous golden robot, its huge arms raised.

Jackson, shirt sleeves rolled above the elbows, was there in the thick of it. Bald head gleaming with sweat, up to his waist in dry grass, brambles and garbage. As he directed with his hands, the JCB reversed, dropped its scoop and thundered forwards.

Bulging rubbish sacks, old fridges and cookers, derelict furniture and beds – the JCB shovelled them up, regardless. Then lifting its arms high, it trundled to a huge lorry parked by the road and tipped its load into the back.

Lee watched. Each time, before allowing the JCB to clear a new section of field, Jackson studied the patch; he scrambled about, lifting, prodding and weighing the debris. Each time, he tested out the ground with his boots, then bent and probed it with his fingers. Only when he'd carried out all these checks, did Jackson wave the driver to go ahead.

'*Lee!*'

He turned. 'Vinda! Roy! . . . Dent!'

The Motleys were followed by Lurch, Anton and Junior . . . then, one by one . . . Jack . . . Grant . . . the other members of the team and a steady trickle of faces from the estate.

Four helmeted men with lances – strimmers: big hand-held grass cutters – had already started to slice deep gashes into the meadow. Several skips had been dropped off along the roadside, ready to be filled with the smaller pieces of rubbish and the chopped vegetation.

The JCB paused in its work.

Jackson came over to have a word with the gathering forces.

'So far, so good!' he said. 'It looks as though the big stuff – fridges, furniture and the like – has only been dumped round the edges.' Taking out a handkerchief, he wiped his shiny dome. 'That's what I'd hoped,' he continued. 'We don't want the weight of the JCB running over what will become the playing area – it wouldn't do the ground any good at all.'

Beyond the strip cleared by the JCB, the real work began. Following the paths cut by the strimmers, Lee put on a pair of gloves and stooped to gather bundles of chopped long grass, weeds and nettles. Behind him others did the same.

They carried the bundles back to the skips. Some of the adults, those with allotments, had brought along tools: a few rakes and a couple of wheelbarrows; everyone else made do with gloves or their hands.

They worked like dogs. Like *mad* dogs. Sunshine blazed down from another bleached sky. From time to time, individuals stopped to rest, to drink, to eat, but the group as a whole kept working.

They continued through into the afternoon and on. Helpers came and went. All sorts joined in.

Between Lee and his teammates there was an unspoken competition: to see who could work the hardest and the longest. Pride was at stake.

Beneath the cut-down grass and weeds lay the rubbish. They uncovered cardboard boxes, newspapers, cans, bottles, buckled bicycle wheels, shoes without heels, dolls with faces defaced and hair pulled out, umbrella skeletons, patent handbags, tennis balls, a cricket ball, punctured footballs, books . . . and clothes enough to dress the entire estate, several times over.

The day wore on. The JCB worked its way right around the field. The lorry, fully laden with the hulks of old fridges and furniture, the burnt-out remains of several mopeds and a car, and the countless bags of garbage, finally drove away with the JCB following behind. As they trundled past, the tired volunteers stopped work to wave and give a cheer.

Skips had been filled, collected and replaced with empty ones which, in their turn, were now almost full. The strimmers had finished their work and gone home. Most of the weeds, the nettles, thorns and brambles had been hacked down, gathered up and thrown in the skips with the rubbish.

Jackson, Lee, the Motleys and a handful of others still remained, now working at little more than a snail's pace.

The sun had lost its heat; it had slipped more than half way down the sky and was gently sinking into the London summer haze. Leaning against a skip, Lee surveyed the brown and yellow patchy mess.

Jackson walked over.

Lee grinned. 'What was that you said? "Nothing quite as beautiful as a well-maintained, freshly mown football pitch" . . .?'

'That's right!' Jackson laughed. 'This is . . .' he shook his head '. . . nothing quite as beautiful as a well-maintained, freshly mown pitch.'

The others joined the laughter.

'We'll see!' said Jackson. 'We don't have long, but we'll see what we can do.'

'What d'you call Brooksie at the end of half-time?' yelled Dent.

'Dunno.'

'Anything you like,' said Dent, 'there's no way he'll catch you.'

Lee felt himself blush. Jackson glanced at him.

'What d'you call a striker that's too out of condition to score goals?' called Vinda.

'Anything you like . . .' said Jackson. 'That's enough of that.'

CHAPTER 14

Together

About to cross the road, Lee paused and stared in surprise as a sleek black limousine cruised past.

This road was always empty. It was the back entrance to the estate – only local people used it.

He followed the car with his eyes. Who could it be? Somebody famous?

He'd travelled in cars like that many times with . . . Dad?!

Lee peered hard after the car. Not Dad . . .? No – Dad wouldn't . . . couldn't, at least not in a car like that, not the way things were going – he'd soon not be able to afford a minicab . . .

Lee shook his head, frowned, kicked the

curb and hurried off across the pitch. Three days ago a big steel freight-container had arrived with the tools and machinery. Now, after days of mowing, watering, rolling and pricking, the ground looked like . . . coarse yellow stubble!

It was patchy in colour and texture, but – Lee smiled to himself – at least it was *flat*.

Tomorrow, Saturday, was their first home match – their second play-off – against Rotherhithe. There was still plenty to be done, but the basic pitch would be ready. The game would get played.

Along with the machinery an old Portakabin had been delivered. It doubled as Jackson's office and a team changing room. Behind it there was a Portaloo.

As Lee jogged towards the team's head-quarters he picked out his teammates: Vinda and Roy, Anton and Lurch, Junior and Jack, Grant, Thomas and Sean. No sign of Dent.

Passing a ball back and forth, the boys chatted and laughed.

Vinda pointed to the road.

Lee looked back. Having turned in the entrance to the estate, the limo was now setting off, back up the road, at the same slow steady speed. He nodded in its direction. 'Do you think someone's lost?'

'Nah!' said Vinda, 'I've seen it before – the same car doing exactly the same thing, a couple of days ago.'

'Word gets about fast,' said Roy. 'Scouts from the premier league have heard whispers about the *fresh* inner-city talent . . .'

There were chuckles from the rest of the team.

'They've heard the reports about an amazing . . .'

'. . . unbelievable . . .'

'. . . wicked . . .'

'. . . *mega* . . .'

'. . . goal of the century!' said Roy. He grinned at Lee.

'Goal of the *millennium*,' said Vinda. 'They've come to sign up Sunningdale's star player, the goal-maker . . .'

Dent stepped out from the Portakabin, behind them.

'– and *scorer* . . .' added Roy.

'. . . *supreme!*' said Vinda.

Vinda and Roy slapped high-five.

'Oh *yeah?*' yelled Dent. 'And who would that be then, *EH?*'

Roy and Vinda glanced at one another.

'You laugh and snigger, you mutter

behind my back, but none of you'll say a word *to my face*! You think it's funny don't you? You can't stop *nattering* about it . . .'

Dent's words echoed off the bleak walls of the estate and back across the silent playing field.

The door of the Portakabin opened. Jackson stepped out behind Dent.

'The goal in question was a team effort,' said Jackson. 'One of the most perfect examples I've witnessed.' He looked from face to face. 'We're a team . . . *let's remember*.' He turned to Dent. 'What matters is that goals are scored, not *who* they're scored by.'

'I *know* that,' snapped Dent. He glowered at the team. 'It's not *me* that keeps going on about it, it's not me that's got the problem . . .'

Nobody spoke.

Twisting round suddenly, Dent pushed past Jackson, stormed inside the Portakabin and slammed the door.

Lee stared. Sheepish faces.

From the corner of his eye he glimpsed a flash of red brake lights. The limo swung out of sight, in the direction of the main road.

'Somebody got out of bed the wrong side,' muttered Lurch.

The others nodded and murmured agreement.

'Talk time!' barked Jackson. He threw open the Portakabin door. 'That includes *you*,' he yelled. 'Out! Now!'

Dent shuffled onto the steps.

'I don't know the rights and wrongs of this . . . *tension*,' said Jackson, 'but I do know it's got to stop.'

He stepped down on to the playing field. 'Team spirit is everything – a team's nothing without it. If we're not working together, we're in *big trouble*. So, whatever your differences and disagreements: sort them out! We train together, we play together – we win . . . *together*.'

Lee brushed his fingers through the dry turf. After two hours of training in the hot sun he was *knackered*!

Jackson had worked them hard. Jackson had worked hard himself – criticizing, encouraging and cracking jokes to lift the team spirit. The man really knew what he was doing.

Lee watched as Jackson explained something to the four defenders. The boys listened intently. Jackson was as good as any Premier division and national squad coaches. He knew – he'd seen them on the job.

Lee turned his attention to Dent – lying flat on his back in the shade.

Once Jackson had got the team started on the exercises proper, Dent had returned to his competitive old self.

Lee smiled to himself.

He and Dent had been teamed together by Jackson for all the exercises which required a partner. They'd tried their hardest to out-perform each other and every other member of the team.

Jackson had finished his discussion with the defenders. He wandered over. 'Dent,' he said, '. . . Lee – good work!' Putting two fingers in his mouth, he whistled.

Boys gathered round.

'There's a good afternoon's work still to be done.' Jackson smiled. 'The pitch has to be watered and rolled, the white lines have to be painted in, the goal posts have arrived and need erecting, nets have to be fitted . . .'

Lee spotted Mum and Tanya making their way down the road from the estate. Even from that distance, he could see they were carrying bags. 'The strip!' he yelled.

Suddenly, the whole team were charging across the pitch, running faster than they had all day.

Lee got there first.

'Don't get excited,' said Mum. 'It's not all finished yet.'

The team crowded round.

From one of the bags she pulled out something blue. 'We've got the shorts,' she said, holding them up. They had two vertical stripes down the hip seams – yellow.

'Not exactly the latest style,' grunted Dent.

'Seventies fashions are all the rage,' chirped Vinda.

Roy laughed. 'We could all get perms and afros!'

'If we weren't on a low budget,' Lee reminded them.

'I'm sure you'd all love something a bit flashier,' said Mum, 'but for the time being – this is practical. You'll look great, all dressed the same for once. They main thing is: it'll make it easier for you to spot each other.'

Tanya rummaged in one of the bags. 'And we've got the socks!' she said. She held up a pair. They were royal blue with two horizontal yellow stripes around the tops.

'The shirts, I'm afraid, will take a while longer,' said Mum, 'they have to be specially printed – there'll be a small logo on the breast.' She held up a pair of socks with a pair of the shorts. 'But at least tomorrow, for the first time, you'll be recognizable as *a team*.'

'And we've got these,' said Tanya, pulling out shin-pads. 'And these!' Ripping open a bag she threw an armful of blue and yellow scarves into the air. 'Now your supporters can wave as well as shout.'

'Excellent!' said Jackson, limping up behind. 'Now all we've got to do is give them something to wave and shout about!'

CHAPTER 15

Sabotage

Lee, Vinda and Roy came panting to a stop.

Jackson was sitting on the Portakabin steps, his face knotted with fury. 'I don't like to swear in front of young people,' he muttered darkly, it was almost a croak, 'but whoever did this . . .'

The three boys exchanged glances, unable to believe the evidence of their eyes. The pitch was peppered with molehills. Dozens of them. Except – they hadn't been made by moles. The mounds of earth sat beside holes which somebody had *dug*.

Lee checked his watch. In ten minutes time, they were supposed to be starting their last training-session before the match. This was a disaster!

'After all our efforts . . .' muttered Roy.

'It wasn't exactly the best quality turf,' said Jackson. He tapped the Portakabin wall. 'And this wasn't the most prestigious pavilion in the world . . .'

The door to the Portakabin was lying on the ground at the bottom of the steps, jagged and splintered where it had been battered from its hinges. All the Portakabin windows had been smashed. 'LOOSERS' had been spray-painted in bright scarlet, several times on each of the outside walls.

Lee climbed the steps and looked inside. Everything had been smashed – tables, chairs, cupboards, sink. Jackson's files – accounts and coaching notes – had all been ripped apart and strewn about. Someone had taken the trouble of tearing the new socks and shorts on something sharp; their shredded remains were heaped in piles.

In a corner underneath one of the broken bench seats, large charred patches on the wall showed where someone had tried to light a fire using the remains of Jackson's notes and the new supporters' scarves.

'The rotten—' hissed Lee.

Vinda and Roy grunted in unison behind him.

'The loo has been damaged, but not smashed,' said Jackson, 'and *thank God*, whoever did this, did *not* manage to get through the padlocks on the container unit.' He shook his head. 'The tools and machinery are safe, at least.'

Junior and Lurch – little and large – made their way across the pitch towards the Portakabin. Behind came Grant, Thomas, Sean, Anton and Jack. They jogged wide-eyed, between the molehills.

'Who would do such a thing . . .?' muttered Jackson, over and over. 'Who would *do* such a thing . . .?'

The faces of the boys showed their shock. Two at a time, they climbed past Jackson and examined the carnage inside the Portakabin. Stepping down to join the others, they stared in gloomy silence at the ruined pitch.

Who would do such a thing?

Jackson's question hung in the air.

Elbows nudged and heads turned.

Lee followed the direction of their gaze.

Dent – hands in pockets, head down, eyes on the ball – was jauntily dribbling his way along the road at the back of the estate. He chipped the ball up on to the pavement.

'Yeah . . .' muttered Lurch. 'Who would do such a thing?'

Dent paused at the edge of the field. He was still a long way off and, at such a distance, it was impossible for anyone at the Portakabin to make out his face. Shielding their eyes from the sun, the Sunningdales peered and squinted.

Lee did the same.

Over on the other side of the field, Dent slowly surveyed the scene. He took a long time.

'Who would do such a thing?' muttered another Sunningdale.

'Yeah.'

Seeming finally to make up his mind, watched by a dozen pairs of eyes, Dent set off at a jog, across the pitch towards the Portakabin.

Lee glanced at his glowering teammates.

Vinda and Roy shrugged.

Lee stared. Surely they didn't think . . .? 'Dent wouldn't do something like this,' he blurted. 'You know he wouldn't!'

'Wouldn't he?' Jackson hadn't moved from the steps. Hand to brow, he stared across the pitch. 'I hope you're right,' he said, 'for all our sakes, I hope you're right.'

Lee squinted. Dent was now running between the 'molehills'.

Ball at his feet, his compact body leant and swerved as he skirted round the mounds of earth. He darted this way and that, turning sharply every time. A virtuoso display of dribbling skills. Now he sprinted.

On the final approach to the Portakabin, he slowed back down to a jog and stopped in front of them. Panting hard, he folded his arms.

Dent searched from face to face. His breathing grew more controlled.

Total silence.

'You lot think I dug up the pitch?' Dent laughed and turned to Jackson.

Then, one after another, to Vinda, Roy and finally – Lee.

'And what about you?' Dent stared at him angrily. 'I suppose you think I did it?'

Lee shook his head. He gestured behind, towards the Portakabin.

Dent frowned. He scratched his neck and stared at the Portakabin. 'You *what*?' he said.

He pushed past Jackson.

They watched.

He looked inside, as each of them had done.

There was a long silence.

Dent slowly shook his head.

'Sunningdale have a match to play,' said Jackson, abruptly getting to his feet. 'How anybody could do such a thing is quite beyond me . . .' He stood at the bottom of the steps. '. . . but we don't have time to start delving into who did this and why – not *right now.*' He was looking up at Dent. 'Tell me you had nothing to do with this . . .'

Dent and Jackson stared into each other's eyes. Dent's gaze flickered momentarily in Lee's direction. Lee wanted to smile, nod, or give some kind of sign . . .

'I was at home all night,' said Dent. 'You can ask my mum.'

Jackson stared so hard, it was like he wanted to look right inside Dent. Slowly, he nodded. 'That's good enough for me. Right!' He clapped his hands. 'All is *not* lost! Time to get to work!'

Lee glanced at Dent. The others had turned away, or were looking at their boots.

'Give me a hand,' he said, crouching

beside the broken door. 'We've got some serious clearing up to do, if we're to make Rotherhithe comfortable.'

'Rotherhithe – comfortable . . .?' Jackson chuckled. 'Now that's going too far!'

CHAPTER 16

Rotherhithe

Whoever had damaged the pitch – they'd not been very smart. Repairing the 'mole-hills' was a simple matter of pushing back the earth that had been piled beside each hole.

More often than not, the pitch's coarse yellowy-brown 'turf' lay in one or two pieces beneath the earth piles. Fitting these back on top of the filled-in holes, Jackson and the boys tamped them down.

By the time Jackson had run the sprinklers for an hour to settle the dust, and gone over everything with the roller, there were less than half a dozen places where the damage was clearly visible.

In the Portakabin, working together,

Lee and Dent cleared away the broken windows, the remains of the door and furniture, the torn-up papers and football kit.

On the outside, Roy and Vinda did their best to cover the graffitti. They had only been able to find white emulsion left over from painting the goal posts and, as their efforts dried, the scarlet lettering began to show through.

Rotherhithe arrived.

The patched-up pitch and Portakabin did not go down well.

'I'm lodging an official complaint with the Sunday Afternoon League!' stormed their coach.

'This isn't Sunningdale's fault,' explained Jackson, politely. 'Vandalism can happen to any club, anywhere. My boys have worked like maniacs all morning to repair the damage. They worked so hard, they left themselves no time for training or a pre-match stretch.'

Softening just a touch at this last piece of news, the visiting team's coach sneered. 'I refuse to let my players use a dilapidated Portakabin marked "loosers" as a changing room. "Loosers" – what's that supposed to mean?'

Jackson smiled. 'You may well ask!'

'Sunningdale's *facilities* beggar the term,' snapped the coach. 'Your pitch is a shambles! You're an insult to the reputation of the league.'

Rotherhithe changed into their all-green strip in the minibuses they'd arrived in.

After their coach had moaned, Rotherhithe and their supporters mocked.

Before the game had even started, a strong chant had built up, echoing against the walls of the estate: *'Sunningdale, Losers . . . Sunningdale, Losers . . . Sunningdale, Losers . . .'*

As Sunningdale, in their rag-bag assortment of kit, ran out from the estate, between the drab grey blocks, Lee found himself thinking of parapets, castle towers and . . . Wembley!

Rotherhithe and their supporters laughed and jeered. Rotherhithe themselves roamed the tired-looking pitch in search of defects. Each time they discovered a darker spot where the ground had clearly been patched, they made a display of stamping down the, already perfectly flat, ground.

Very funny.

'A warm welcome to our visitors!'

announced Jackson, through the small loudspeaker, 'The first, we hope, of many.'

Sunningdale were playing at home and a large crowd had turned out to cheer.

Jackson apologized to the visiting team for the lack of facilities, and to the home supporters for the lack of team strip and colours. He explained briefly about the vandalism, holding up for all to see: the torn remains of a pair of socks, a pair of shorts and a supporter's scarf. 'Further contributions to pitch, pavilion and strip funds will, of course,' he added, 'be gratefully received.'

From their kick-off, Rotherhithe launched a series of fast and furious attacks, pushing for immediate advantage.

But they found themselves blocked.

Again and again, Sunningdale's defence stubbornly resisted.

After a few minutes, the visitors settled down to something a little less frantic. The game proceeded at a more measured pace – both sides playing with a degree of caution, as they tried to assess the strengths and weaknesses of their opponents.

Dent, as ever, led his side from the front.

But the week's intensive team-training seemed to amount to nothing. Communication had vanished. Time and again Sunningdale lost the ball.

'What on earth's wrong with you lot!' yelled Dent. 'What happened to working together?!'

Turning around one of Sunningdale's early advances, Rotherhithe showed a dangerous ability to counter-attack with rapid sprints back into the home side's half.

In spite of Dent's furious reprimands to his forwards, each time Rotherhithe repeated the tactic, they caught the Sunningdales napping. Under increasing pressure, Roy was producing heroic saves.

Lee found himself yo-yo-ing back and forth, from attack-support to defence.

There was a muggy heat, the air was warm and heavy, it was hard to breathe; neither side could sustain a push for very long. Possession swung from one team to the other, then back again.

Lee kept running.

Rotherhithe were the dominant side. Sunningdale were all over the place, struggling to fight a rear-guard action.

Twice in quick succession, Rotherhithe's

blitzkriegs almost resulted in goals.

Lee had been forced to hang back, to prevent the visitors getting through. He found himself backing up his captain's calls with his own furious shouts.

'Come on, Sunningdale,' he yelled. 'Get behind your captain. Work *together*!'

He made it his job to go for every loose ball or Rotherhithe player that crossed the half-way line. He couldn't intercept every one – that was down to teamwork – but he tackled and worried as many as he could.

It was hard, frustrating work.

When the whistle blew at the end of the first half, Lee breathed a heavy sigh of relief.

No score. Sunningdale had got off lightly.

Tanya and Lee's mum brought over the much-needed drinks, then departed.

Sitting and crouching, the team stretched in front of their goal.

Dent had sauntered over to the far side, to join the Portaloo queue.

Lee got to his feet. 'What is *wrong* with you lot!'

Handing round towels, Jackson stopped and stared.

'Perhaps it's not my place . . .' said Lee.

Jackson shook his head. 'No . . . please – go ahead . . .'

'I just don't get it – did everything we've learnt at Charnley and in our practices go out the window?' His hands were waving helplessly. 'What happened to teamwork? What happened to looking out for one another? What happened to *getting behind your captain*?'

Most of the team were staring at the ground. A couple of them looked over towards Dent, in the Portaloo queue.

'Oh, I get you . . .' said Lee. '. . . this is all about the vandalism. You still think it was Dent – is that it?' He looked around. 'Because of his little outburst?' He turned to Vinda. 'Well?' Then to Roy. 'What's the problem?' he demanded. 'Can't one of you speak?'

Nobody would meet his gaze.

'*Well?*'

No answer.

Jackson surveyed the faces.

Lee clenched his fists. 'Listen – if we don't win this match, we're out of the play-offs. We're *finished*.' He looked around. 'Most of you know Dent better than me. Do you really think he'd destroy the team he's done so much to build?'

Lee pointed to the Portaloo; Dent was inside.

'This match he's been killing himself, trying to make something happen. And he's had *zero* support from the rest of you . . .'

All eyes were down.

'If Dent had done all that damage on his own,' said Lee, 'it would've taken him half the night – so how come he's played with more energy than the rest of you put together?'

'If Dent didn't do it,' said Roy, 'who did?'

'*There* might lie our answer,' said Jackson. He pointed.

The team sat up and stared.

Lee followed their gaze.

A sleek black shape emerged from behind the parked minibuses and cars of the visiting supporters. It cruised slowly to the end of the road.

Who was in the limo?

'Talent scouts again!'

Heads turned.

Dent came running towards them.

'Talent scouts?' Jackson chuckled and shook his head. 'Councillors, more like, or property developers . . .' He bowed his head. 'Dent, I'm afraid we all . . .' He hesitated and glanced at Lee. 'One person excluded . . . we all owe you an apology.'

Dent smiled.

The feeling was electric.

'We've got them on the run!' Lee yelled. 'Come *on*! Now we're *really* playing like a team!'

In the space of twenty minutes, Sunningdale had come back from their lousy first half with *three* beautifully crafted goals. One to Vinda, two for Dent.

All solid team efforts – built from deep within their own half.

With supporters yelling at virtual *fever pitch*, the home crowd had swollen by the minute. Residents were running back from the estate to see what all the noise and excitement was about.

Lee felt his smile in his heart. No doubt about it – Sunningdale were dominating the second half. Inspired play and brilliant teamwork!

'Work together!'

Again and again, Lee egged on his teammates, echoing his captain's call.

'Come on—' he yelled. 'Keep watching for each other!'

Rotherhithe had seldom managed to get the ball away since the start of the second half. When they did, Sunningdale's defence had been there to meet them. The visitors' strategy seemed to have dissolved; every player was a defender – that's all there was to it. Sunningdale had them on the run.

And their supporters wanted more.

'We want more – we want four!' they yelled from the touchline. *'We want more – we want four!'*

He had stayed back all this time, keeping an eye out for kick-and-run attacks. But now – Sunningdale had gelled so well and were three goals ahead. Now – there was less than ten minutes left before the whistle.

It was the moment to join the attack.

'Yours!' yelled Dent, passing the ball back.

Lee moved forwards slowly, taking his time on the ball. There was no immediate danger.

Once again, Rotherhithe were falling back, rather than coming out to meet them.

Lee looked around, checking the positions of his teammates. He couldn't help

grinning. For things to have turned
around this well . . . *brilliant*!

There was room to build up speed on the
approach.

At the very last minute, he lofted the
ball to Vinda, way out left, then accelerated.

Charging into the penalty area, weaving
between Rotherhithe, he popped up in a
space close to the farside post.

Dent was in a sea of green shirts. Lurch
was there too, on the outskirts of the box.
Anton, Junior and Grant were coming to
join the fray.

The ball from Vinda was already in the
air. Rotherhithe and Sunningdales alike
were leaping skyward as it came across.
Dent was in perfect position.

Dent twisted. 'Yours!' he yelled.

Lee sprang.

He soared.

He *scored*.

'What a *cracker*!'

Coming up behind, Dent gave him a
quick, stiff, hug. 'Another beauty!'

'Thanks!' Lee grinned.

They jogged back to the centre.

In the middle of a tight little group,

patting each other on the back, Lee suddenly stopped.

It was a new chant.

The full-time whistle blew.

'*Sunningdale U-ni-ted! Sunningdale U-ni-ted! Sunningdale U-ni-ted!*'

Nothing else could be heard.

CHAPTER 17

Limo

Jackson insisted – Sunday was to be completely restful. No football. No work.

After a day off lolling and loafing, Monday morning saw Lee teamed up with Dent and Anton door-knocking on the estate. The smashed-up Portakabin furniture needed replacing. Everybody on the estate had heard about the vandalism and Sunningdale's victory over Rotherhithe. The donations came thick and fast.

By the time the three boys had carted the chairs and table to the Portakabin, Vinda and Roy had finally managed to obliterate the misspelt graffiti. Inside and out, the Portakabin's walls glowed whiter than white.

Jack, Junior, Sean, Thomas and Grant had been working alongside Jackson – checking the pitch for unevenness where holes had been filled, helping him roll and water.

When the full squad had arrived, Jackson gathered the boys in front of the Portakabin.

'After we'd paid out for the pitch-clearing and team strip,' said Jackson, 'there was very little money left. We don't have the funds to put up fencing, lights, alarms or any of that sort of stuff . . . I've been thinking about what we could do to prevent further vandalism.'

Unfolding a piece of paper, Jackson pinned it to the door. 'Take a look at this.'

The squad crowded round.

Lee pushed forward.

Mr S.J. Thomson,
Secretary, South-East Region,
Sunday Afternoon League

Mr Jackson, Coach,
Sunningdale Under-Fourteens.

Dear Mr Jackson,
Following Saturday's second-round

matches, I received a phone call from the Rotherhithe UF coach – Mr Burke.

Mr Burke complained of 'rude treatment', 'third world facilities' and 'a patchwork-quilt pitch' at Sunningdale, and insisted these factors gave the home side 'unfair advantages'.

In light of Rotherhithe's 4–0 defeat, I am inclined to treat these allegations with some scepticism. However, SAL's official complaints procedure must be followed. I am, therefore, writing to inform you that before the final play-off this forthcoming Saturday, I shall be inspecting Sunningdale's pitch and facilities.

In the event that pitch and facilities are indeed found to be below the standards required by the league, the second-round result would have to be nullified and the final called off. A new final would then be scheduled, with Rotherhithe taking the place forfeited by Sunningdale.

I hope this will not be necessary.

In the meantime, it is my more pleasant duty to inform you that,

*assuming Saturday's final play-off
still goes ahead:*

*1) Your opponents will be your near
neighbours – Grovesnor YFC.*

*2) I shall be on hand to announce
the team who go through to* SAL's
Under-Fourteens Division.

*I look forward to meeting you and
Sunningdale on the day.*

Yours sincerely

Mr S.J. Thomson
SAL *Secretary, South-East Region*

Voices groaned.
'*Grovesnor!*'
'We might as well give up now.'
'I can't believe I'm hearing this!' snapped
Lee. 'We're a completely changed side from
the one that lost to Grovesnor . . . lots has
happened since then – we've been training,
we've been winning . . .'
'Yeah,' muttered someone, 'and now it's
all coming to an end.'
'Right now, *that* isn't what concerns us.'
Jackson unfolded a second piece of paper.
'Any further damage to the pitch and

Portakabin and we could be in trouble. If Mr Thomson decides things aren't up to scratch, all our good work *will* have been for nothing – we won't have the chance to prove ourselves on the pitch . . .'

Jackson handed the paper to Lee.

The squad crowded round.

'"Five-thirty sharp!"' read Lee. '"Tuesday – Vinda, Roy and Lurch, Wednesday – Anton, Grant and Sean, Thursday—"'

'What's this?!' said Dent.

Jackson nodded towards the Portakabin. 'For the next five days, I'm sleeping in here. At five-thirty every morning, three of the team must be at the Portakabin to take over guard-duty whilst I grab a few hours kip. For the rest – it's nine o'clock as usual.'

'Do we wake you?' asked Lee.

Jackson smiled. 'Each night, I'll write out a list of tasks and who's to do what. When you arrive in the morning, you can get on with it. After all your jobs are finished, you start the jog. If I haven't surfaced by the time that's over, wake me – tea with two sugars!'

Panting, Lee glanced at his watch – 10.15 a.m.

The day had started with a jolt and the alarm's *bleep-bleep-bleep* five hours ago! It had been his and Dent's turn to relieve Jackson. No wonder he felt sluggish.

Sweat stung his eyes.

There were still two more laps of the jog to go; the rest of the team were laughing about his and Dent's struggle to keep up.

Vinda chuckled at the front of the pack. 'Don't look now – but there's that limo!'

Lee glanced across the pitch.

Ahead of him, Anton, Roy and Lurch bumped against each other, stumbled and almost fell.

'Come *on*!' yelled Dent. 'Look where you're going! Forget about the mystery car and *concentrate*!'

The pack rounded the corner and headed up behind the goal line.

By the time they'd reached the pavement's edge, the limo had passed and was turning in the estate entrance.

The pack turned left, back towards the Portakabin. They were growing nervy, pushing the pace.

'Ease up!' yelled Dent.

'There's another lap yet,' added Lee, wiping the sweat from his forehead. He fought the temptation to look back.

The velvet throb of the limousine's engine grew louder and louder. Inch by inch, the sleek black shape pulled past.

Lee snatched a glance.

The pack accelerated.

The limousine's purr rose a notch.

Suddenly, the pack were *sprinting*. This was a race!

Lee gasped for air, his arms and legs pumping like pistons.

The limo surged. It pulled ahead – faster and faster – roaring towards the end of the road.

His legs were *burning*.

Level with the Portakabin, the limo braked. Tyres screeched, two wheels bumped up onto the pavement, dust billowed.

Blood thumped in Lee's ears. The pack had slowed to little more than a jog.

He peered through the cloud of dust around the limousine.

The rear door swung open. A large, dark-suited figure climbed out.

'Lads!'

He was huge, like a bull – cropped hair, no neck and massive shoulders. His voice boomed effortlessly.

'*Lads!*' He stretched out both arms, blocking their path like a giant. Heavy-lidded eyes glinted. 'We need to talk . . .'

Jostling each other like panicky sheep, the Sunningdales held back.

Lee eased forward. He sensed Dent pushing through beside him.

'Some of you probably recognize me,' said the big man. 'I used to live on the estate.'

Dent nodded. 'Tyler's dad . . .'

'That's right!' The big man gave a hearty chuckle. 'Your local representative on the council.'

Lee glared at Dent. Jackson had mentioned . . .

'*This,*' boomed the big man, gesturing in the direction of the playing field, '. . . is *council property.*'

Lee swallowed. All of a sudden he was feeling shaky.

'Whose idea was it?!' snapped the big man.

Dent glanced at Lee. Behind them, the others shuffled and lowered their eyes.

'Mine . . .' said Lee.

'*Ours* . . .' Dent pointed at Lee. 'His and mine.'

The big man glowered. Slowly, he shook

his head. '*Bad* idea! Your local council had plans for this land. People can't just go taking what doesn't belong to them!'

'No-one was using it,' said Lee. 'There's nowhere else to play football.'

'*Nowhere else to play!?!*' The big man guffawed. 'What about the tarmac pitch? My son and his friends have played happily down there for years.'

Lee held back a snort of derision. A loud-mouthed thug, and a fat monster and a deranged maniac . . . hurling abuse and metal bars, smashing bottles, hacking-up tarmac, using a dead rat as a football . . . hardly five-year-olds playing in a sand-pit! He *had to* answer back, say *something* . . . He shook his head. 'Vandalizing scum!'

The big man's eyes narrowed and glared. Lee shivered.

Beside him, Dent grunted. 'Talk of the devil!'

The bull head twisted. 'All right, boys!'

Nodding coolly, Tyler, Tubs and Sky crossed over the road and took up positions on either side of the big man.

Lee felt Dent shifting uneasily. Eight evil eyes stared.

The big man nodded towards the pitch. 'Your activities have to cease!'

'*Cease!*' whispered Tyler. He grinned, enjoying the threat in the word.

Lee chewed the inside of his lip.

'You're holding up progress . . .' said the big man.

'We can't have that!' sneered Tyler.

Lee was frantic – he wanted to shout them down . . . but he was *terrified*.

He tried to steady his thoughts. He tried to form words in his mouth.

From somewhere between his throat and the back of his nose came a loud snorting noise.

The eyes glared.

Every pore in his skin felt like a laser burn.

'More d-d-digging then . . .?' he blurted.

Dent shuffled his feet beside him. The others fidgeted nervously behind.

'. . . And d-d-decorating?' said Dent. 'At the d-dead of night?'

Fists clenched.

Tyler snarled.

The big man's eyes bulged. His face turned purple.

Lee could hear himself thinking inside his head, wondering what else he could say . . . He could hear the individual thrumps of his heartbeat in his ears . . .

'You should give these boys a chance, *Councillor.*'

Everybody turned.

Jackson!

He strode towards them from the Portakabin. 'They've worked themselves into the ground for their team.'

The big man gaped, like he'd seen a ghost.

Tyler frowned.

The big man puffed out his chest and drew himself up to his full height.

'You've seen the crowds they draw,' said Jackson. 'Close them down, and there could be calls for an enquiry . . .' He stepped up close.

The big man seemed to lean back a little, uncomfortably.

'Awkward questions might be asked . . . things might be recalled which you would rather were left unsaid . . . *Councillor* . . .'

The big man's nostrils flared; his face turned a more furious purpley-red. 'Are you *THREATENING* me?' he roared.

Jackson didn't budge or blink. 'I have a suggestion . . .'

Turning, he put an arm each around Lee

and Dent's shoulders. 'If this team get into the league, the council allows them to continue using the pitch . . .'

The big man squeezed his hands and cracked his knuckles. His shoulders hunched.

He wants to pulverize Jackson, thought Lee, *then strangle him!*

'*Councillor* . . .' Jackson spoke firmly. 'You're used to having your own way . . . but I suggest, for once – *you listen!*'

Folding his arms, the big man grunted.

'If Sunningdale qualify for the league,' said Jackson, 'the council must agree to provide another pitch for the team if they still want to develop this land . . .' He nodded towards the estate. '. . . for example, by resurfacing the old tarmac pitch with Astroturf . . .'

The big man glowered.

'If Sunningdale lose they give up the playing field. The council goes ahead with its plans – no interference.'

'No awkward questions?!' The big man scowled. 'No calls for any enquiries?'

'Not another squeak.'

'You lose – you give it up?!' The big man gestured towards the pitch and Portakabin.

'The whole shooting-match . . . lock stock and barrel?'

'That's right.'

Lee stared. What was Jackson doing! What was he saying!?

The big man frowned. Tyler leant close and whispered. The manic eyes were staring past Jackson . . . past Dent and Lee . . .

Before Lee could even twist . . .

'Hiya!' Tanya's chirp. Skipping up beside him, she grabbed his hand.

Tyler's frown darkened; slowly, a hint of a smile twisted up the corners of his mouth.

Lee felt a shiver down his spine.

Eyes glued to Tanya, Tyler nudged Tubs and whispered. Tubs' eyes widened. He nodded.

Lee jerked Tanya's arm. '*What are you doing here . . .?*' he hissed.

She gave a start. 'Mum sent me . . .'

He squeezed her hand. '*Shhh!*' His eyes were glued to the big man and his bully boys. They were staring right at Tanya.

'I'm waiting . . .' reminded Jackson.

An ugly smile crept across the big man's

face. 'All right . . . you lose – you leave!' he growled.

'But if we win,' said Jackson, 'the pitch is ours.'

The big man held out his fat hand. A gold watch and rings glittered in the sun. 'Deal!'

Jackson nodded. 'A man's as good as his word . . .'

Lee sat at the Portakabin table, sharing sandwiches with Tanya, Jackson and Dent.

Some of the team were outside; others had gone to the shops, or home to get lunch.

'I don't get it,' said Lee. 'Why say we'll hand back the pitch if we lose?'

'Councillor Tyler has to think he could win,' said Jackson.

'He can!' Dent kicked the wall. 'This old box might be on the scrap heap a week from now.'

'And us!' said Lee.

'O ye of little faith!' Jackson leaned towards them conspiratorially.

Lee, Dent and Tanya exchanged glances.

'The whole thing was a bluff!' Jackson put a finger to his lips. 'The truth is – I

have no evidence. I know Councillor Tyler took bribes, but I can't *prove* it. He knows he treated me shabbily, and he knows I was around when he was setting up his dodgy deals . . . I might have something on him, I might not . . . he can't be sure . . .'

Lee glanced at Tanya, eagerly unwrapping a chocolate roll. 'I'm worried . . .' he said.

'They're planning something . . .' said Dent.

Jackson frowned. 'You can be sure of that . . . I wouldn't put anything past them. The pitch and Portakabin are taken care of, but from now on . . .' he gave the slightest nod towards Tanya, '. . . we must be vigilant at all times.'

CHAPTER 18

Chat

In the days leading up to the start of the new football season, newspaper sports pages grew crowded with articles about the leading clubs, players and managers. In column after column, the writers speculated about what performances the new season might bring.

Lee could feel the pre-season excitement in his bones. He was antsy . . .

On errands to the local shop, he loitered by the newspaper shelf, glancing at back-page headlines, pictures and occasionally . . . articles.

Every day there was something about Brooksie. Sometimes there were several pieces and still – hardly a fact between them. Brooksie was at a health farm . . . he was in a rehabilitation clinic . . . he'd been spotted in a betting shop . . . spotted in a casino . . . he worked behind the counter in a chip shop . . . he'd been sold to a European club . . . he'd already left the country . . .

The photos were grim and fuzzy – a figure getting into a car or getting out . . . peering from behind curtains . . . peeping from dark doorways. The appearance varied from photo to photo, but in all of them, the man – with and without a beard – was dressed in hats, dark glasses and baggy ill-fitting clothes.

The stories made the knot in Lee's stomach tighten, but he couldn't stop reading them. There were as many articles about Brooksie as dealt with all the other players put together. And not one good word about him.

Taking the long route, Lee sauntered back from the shops, skimming the articles he had bought the paper for: Brooksie's transfer fee was embarrassingly low . . . his manager denied he was up for transfer . . . his manager wouldn't say whether or not he'd be playing at the start of the season if he played, he'd be the laughing-stock . . .

. . . wasn't Brooksie finished? Did anyone in their right mind expect him to play in the premier division again?

'Hey – *dribbler*!'

Lee jerked round. Tyler! Right behind him, with Tubs and Sky.

Tyler stepped closer. 'Dribbler . . . what's the difference between Brooksie . . . and a sack of potatoes?'

Lee stared, paralysed. *Just another innocent Brooksie joke?*

Tyler stared back.

Lee felt his lips moving, but no sound came out. He swallowed. 'A couple of stone . . .?'

Tubs and Sky stared expectantly.

Lee shrugged. His eyes were glued to Tyler's face. The face darkened, the mouth opened, the eyes glinted . . .

Tyler *howled*.

Lee's heart tried to kick its way out of his chest.

Tyler was laughing!

Lee shivered – from relief or fear, he couldn't tell.

'Clever!' said Tyler. '*Very* clever . . .' He snatched the paper from Lee's hands. 'Keeping an eye on the footie?'

Lee dug his fingers into his thighs, to

stop them shaking. He wanted to run. He willed himself to.

'I thought we might have a little chat . . .' said Tyler.

'Actually,' said Lee, glancing at his watch. 'I'm in a bit of a hurry!'

'Oh – that's a shame!'

Lee shrugged. He began to twist . . .

Something hard clamped his shoulder.

'Before you go . . .'

The grip tightened. Tyler breathed close to his ear.

'That little girl – Tanya? – your sister, is she?'

Lee belted. Legs pumping. He ran. Down walkways. Up stairwells. He ran blindly. Ran until he was gasping and his lungs felt like they would rip his chest apart . . .

He was lost. The walkways all looked the same. He ran on. Suddenly, he saw a door . . .

'What did I say?' Jackson pushed the front door shut.

'". . . be vigilant at all times . . ."' Panting, Lee stared at the carpet.

'So much for an old man's advice! Well . . .?'

Lee shrugged.

'What did they do?' Jackson limped towards him. 'What did they say?'

He shrugged again. 'Just some things . . .'

'What sort of things?'

'Tyler asked me about Tanya . . .'

'What did he say?'

'He asked if she was my sister . . .'

Jackson frowned. 'Anything else?'

'He asked me a joke . . .'

'A joke?! What about?'

Lee sneaked a glance. Jackson was watching him. '. . . Brooksie.'

'And . . .?'

Lee stared at the carpet again. 'I'd heard it before . . .'

Jackson put a hand on his shoulder.

'That was it?'

'He nicked my newspaper.'

'He didn't hurt you?'

'No.'

Lee lay back against the cushions and closed his eyes. His frantic heartbeat had slowed, but still it sounded loud enough to be heard outside the room.

'Lee . . .?' Jackson spoke from the kitchen. 'Can I ask you something?'

Lee tensed – that question always meant trouble. 'You can ask . . .'

'How did you feel after the auction?'

'OK . . .' His voice sounded flat. '. . . I felt *good*.' He tried to force a smile into it. 'I'm *glad* I did it.'

Jackson carried in two mugs. 'Gift from your dad?'

Lee turned away. The heartbeat quickened again.

'It's all right.' Jackson held out the mug. 'You don't want to talk about him, I know . . .'

Lee gave a start. 'You know?!'

'I *understand*,' said Jackson. 'I mean – I know what it's like . . .'

'Oh . . .'

'I was a son once, believe it or not.' As Jackson lowered himself into the armchair, his knees made a horrible cracking sound. 'I've been a father too.'

Lee sipped his tea. 'What happened to your wife?'

'We got divorced . . .' Jackson gazed into his mug. '. . . nearly thirty years ago. My daughter's a grown-up woman – not unlike your mum.'

He shook his head and smiled. 'Tricky business – being a father. As kids we grow

176

up thinking our dads are gods. Then, when we find they're not . . . . when we find they've got flaws and faults . . . and they *get old* . . .' Jackson stretched out his legs in front of him. The knees crunched again. 'Yep! – even soccer stars wear out and grow old.'

Lee stared into his mug.

'It went for a great price . . . the foot-ball . . .'

'Yeah!' Lee sighed. 'You said it would . . .'

'Ah-ha!' Jackson tapped the end of his nose. 'Inside information!' His eyes twinkled. 'I got chatting to a bloke at the Charnley match. He told me he was a collector – football memorabilia. That's when I got the idea to sell off some of my stuff for the cause.'

'You were really generous,' said Lee.

'No more than you.'

Lee shook his head. 'It's different.'

'Anyway,' said Jackson, 'I invited the bloke along, thinking I might get a better price and blow me . . .'

'Mum beat him to it!'

Jackson nodded. 'But I'm glad I invited him – it was him that bought your foot-ball . . .'

Lee felt the hairs bristle on the back of his neck.

Jackson chuckled. '. . . the man in the hat.'

'Mr Thomson has given the pitch the OK . . .'

'Good . . .' Mum nodded, but she wasn't really listening. Pulling a polythene-wrapped package, a bright swirl of blue and gold, from one of two large boxes, she frowned. 'I don't understand . . .'

Lee stared.

'There's a note from the manufacturer,' said Mum. '"An anonymous supporter, asked us to produce a second strip, plus scarves et cetera . . . for the team . . . and have them delivered with the original order . . . A design was provided and the order paid for in cash . . . I trust *all* the enclosed will be to your satisfaction."'

Taking out one of the shirts, Lee held it next to one of the cheaper, plainer ones they had ordered. The second strip was made up from the same shades of blue and gold as the original – there the similarities ended. It was radically patterned; it was stylish. It was *cool*.

The shirts were printed with dots and swirls, up the sleeves and across the shoulders, like the strips of some professional clubs. On the back was a circle made up of one, two, three . . . Lee counted . . . *eleven* hands inter-linked. In the middle of the circle, on each shirt, the player's number; and in bold, slanted letters across the chest, the words SUNNINGDALE UNITED.

'*Mega!*' he said. 'These must have cost *a fortune.*'

Mum nodded. She had ripped her way into the second box. 'And look,' she said. 'Scarves and baseball caps in the team colours.' She scooped up a bundle. Each of them had 'Sunningdale United' printed in the same style of writing. 'There's *loads*!' she said. 'This is fantastic! The supporters will love them!'

'Talent scouts are rumoured to be interested . . .' said Lee. '*Someone* must think we've got great potential.' He held up one of the shirts, against himself. Star quality or what! 'When the team see these,' he said, 'they are going to go *crazy*!'

CHAPTER 19

Attack

Why was he going ahead with this?

Every time the bus stopped, Lee pressed himself further into the seat. The number 12 route still had the old open-backed buses; it would be so easy to get up and jump off. He could cross the road and catch another straight back home to the Sunningdale Estate . . .

A fat black woman jammed an enormous shopping bag between the two seats and squeezed herself in, crushing him further into his corner. She heaved a second huge bag onto her lap. Lee braced himself against the window. The woman frowned and muttered; her elbow jabbed him in the ribs.

He turned his face towards the cool glass. They were nearing the West End. Suddenly, the view opened out – the grey waters of the Thames flanked by grand buildings and office blocks. The bus was crossing Westminster bridge.

He felt his heart flutter – it wouldn't be long now.

Dad had sounded surprised on the phone: surprised to get the call, but *pleased*. The conversation had been difficult – both of them nervous and in a hurry to hang up.

The arrangement to meet had been hasty. Dad had suggested St James' Park – the place where they'd fed the ducks last Christmas.

A lone figure leant propped against the railing; something about the stance was familiar. Lee craned his neck and peered. He recognized the black baseball cap and baggy blue jacket.

He checked his watch – twelve o'clock midday – from Trafalgar Square, it had taken less than five minutes. Concentrating on taking slow, deep breaths, he commanded his legs to keep walking. Forwards.

Dad spotted him and waved.

They walked towards each other.

Dad smiled as they drew close. 'You found it all right, then?'

Lee shrugged.

Dad nudged his Ray-Bans back to the bridge of his nose and shuffled awkwardly from one foot to the other.

Lee stuffed his hands in his pockets.

Suddenly, leaning forwards, Dad pecked him on the cheek. It was hurried and clumsy; their faces bumped. Dad was clean-shaven.

'Sorry!' Dad touched his arm. He pointed to a nearby refreshments kiosk. 'Let's get something to drink . . . then we can find somewhere more private.'

Dad started to head off, then stopped and span round. 'Sorry – I should have asked . . .' He frowned. 'What do *you* want to do?'

Dad's car stood in the shade of a tall tree, separated from the park by a low rail and bushes.

From the passenger seat, Lee gazed out through the windscreen. Tourists, secretaries and businessmen – jackets off, buttons undone – flopped into deckchairs, or kicked off their shoes and laid down on the grass to enjoy the sunshine.

Lee shifted in the seat. He couldn't get comfortable. Suggesting they sit in the car had seemed like a good idea, but now he and Dad were here, it felt awkward.

He was glad Dad had offered to sit in the back for extra leg room. At least they weren't right next to each other, they didn't have to keep twisting to look at each other – that would have been *unbearable*.

Adjusting the rear-view mirror, Lee glanced.

Dad sipped from a bottle of fizzy mineral water. The sunglasses made it impossible to tell where he was looking.

Lee dropped his gaze. The knot in his stomach was tight. He took a swig of cola. *What had he wanted to say?*

'It's really difficult . . .' he croaked. He swallowed more cola to clear his throat.

'That's OK,' Dad's voice was neutral, 'we've got time . . . there's no rush . . .' He sipped. 'I'm glad you wanted to talk.'

'You've not exactly made it easy . . .' Lee felt his breath shudder. 'I mean . . .' He glanced in the mirror. Was Dad staring behind those glasses? Was he listening?

He felt himself begin to tremble.

'Because of *you*,' he blurted, 'the last twelve months have been total *hell*.' He whacked the dashboard with his fist. 'You've *ruined* everything . . . spoilt *everything*!'

Anger and sadness tugged at his guts.

'How could you do that? I don't understand . . . How could you let everybody down – the club, the country, the supporters . . .'

He gulped. His chest heaved.

'. . . Mum and Tanya . . . me . . .'

'Lee—'

'. . . how *could* you?'

His voice had risen, it was shaky. He couldn't stop now.

'I mean . . . I can't understand – one minute you were this . . . *cool dad* – teaching me stuff about fair play and self-respect – the next, you're doing the opposite of everything you ever told me, acting like a complete . . .'

His breath came in little short gasps. *How come there was no air all of a sudden?* He wound down the window a crack.

'You've become what you taught me to *despise* . . .' he gasped. 'You . . .'

'What . . .?' Dad spoke softly.

184

Lee's lungs heaved and shuddered, his chest felt like it would explode. '... You ...'

'Go on, Lee ...' There was no anger in Dad's voice, just gentle urging. '... *say it!*'

'... You drink too much ...'

Dad nodded.

'... you're out of condition ...'

Dad nodded again.

'... and you *lie* ...' His lungs made a loud wheezing noise. '... you've become ... a *loser*.' There was no air. His lungs emptied out with a rasping, bubbling sound and his shoulders locked. '*Heuuaaa-a-a-a-agh!*' He gasped. He coughed. He lurched forward.

'*Lee!*'

He felt a hand on his shoulder.

His chest ... his lungs were ... locked tight ... crushing him ... he couldn't ... *breathe* ...

'*Heuuaaa-a-a-a-gh!*'

'*Lee!*'

The hand pulled him back.

'*Lee* – where's your inhaler?'

Lee shook his head. He'd never had one. This had never happened before.

'*Lee—*' Dad's voice was close by his ear. '*Lee* – breathe through your hands!'

Lee felt Dad's arm round his shoulders.

He cupped his hands to his mouth. His lungs hurt. His breath felt warm and moist on his fingers.

Dad rubbed his back. 'Keep breathing . . . come on . . . through your hands – that's it . . . try to relax . . .'

'*Heuuaaah!*' Lee gave a little cough. Something loosened. He panted for air.

'I used to f-f-feel *so proud!*' he blurted. He was shaking. 'Being Brooksie's son felt like . . . the best thing that could ever happen!'

He coughed some more.

'I never used to boast. I didn't need to – everybody knew who you were. And they called me "Brooksie" too.'

The dashboard was wobbling. Lee wiped away tears.

'I was good and I was *so* confident; it was like nothing could touch me . . .'

'Then I let you down . . .' Dad's voice was barely more than a croak.

Lee nodded. He took a deep, quivering breath. 'I *hated* you . . .' He wiped his nose. 'I felt so *ashamed* . . .'

Lee gazed through the windscreen. Sunlight sparkled on the lake. The tears had gone. His breathing was steady.

For some time, Dad hadn't moved in the back. He hadn't spoken.

'It's Tanya that has an inhaler,' said Lee.

Dad made a tutting noise. 'How stupid of me . . .' The baseball cap bobbed as he frowned.

Lee sighed.

Dad sighed.

They both sighed together.

'Anything else you want to get off your chest?' said Dad.

Lee jerked round, scowling.

'Sorry!' Dad put up a hand. 'I wasn't trying to be funny . . . sometimes that's what happens, if people don't get a chance to talk about what's bothering them.'

'They have asthma attacks?' said Lee.

Dad nodded. 'You'd be surprised!' He eased himself back into the rear seat. 'Get it all out . . .' he said. '*Tell* me . . .'

Lee bit his lip. 'I feel stronger,' he said. 'Not just *now*, I mean – since we moved away.'

Silence from the back.

'At first . . . after we left, it felt really hard. But it's got better. *I've* got better . . .'

He glanced in the rear-view mirror. No movement.

'All those times you coached me, trained with me and explained stuff to me . . . I suppose I just want to *remind* you.'

Dad's face twitched.

'Over and over, you used to tell me: ". . . you can have all the talent and all the training in the world, but, in the end, it's down to *confidence*." That's what you used to say. Confidence creates luck. Confidence is *king*. Find your confidence, then . . .' He made the clenched fist Dad always used to make. 'Make it hard, like *stone*.'

He paused. The knot in his stomach tightened.

'When you lost it – I lost it too. But now . . . my confidence is *mine*.'

Dad's face twitched again.

Lee watched. 'Now,' he said, 'I think I understand what you meant.'

Dad gave the tiniest of nods.

'Everyone wants to see you get back on your feet . . . I know they do . . .'

A muffled coughing sound came from the back.

He bit his lip, tasting blood. 'Everyone . . . except maybe the newspapers.'

In the back, Dad turned away.

'Thanks . . .' he croaked. 'Do I get a turn now?'

Lee nodded.

'What I've got to say will need to be kept quiet . . .' said Dad, '. . . for forty-eight hours or so . . .'

Lee nodded. 'OK.'

Dad slipped off the sunglasses, pulled off the baseball cap and began to unzip his jacket.

Lee twisted round. Dad's hair was short and neatly cut. He looked . . . *different*.

Dad smiled.

Leaning between the seats, Lee stared closer. Dad's eyes were slightly glassy, the rims were a touch pinkish, but otherwise – clear and bright! No red rings, no puffy black bags . . .

Dad grinned and rubbed his eyes. 'It's just emotions!' he said. 'I've not touched a drop. I've been eating proper food and I've *not* been miserable or depressed.'

He hoisted up his T-shirt. The stomach wasn't exactly muscley . . . but it wasn't fat. He laughed. 'I've trained *hard* every day for the last three weeks and I feel great!'

Lee stared.

'Something clicked . . .' said Dad, '– that last time . . . when we all met up at the café in the shopping centre? I saw how much everything was getting to you . . .'

Lee felt his breath tremble.

'We hadn't spoken for so long . . .' said Dad. 'I saw your rage . . . pent-up . . . *seething* . . .' He smiled. 'It got to me . . .'

Lee shuddered.

'I came to watch Sunningdale play.'

Lee jolted. '*What!*'

'It's all right!' said Dad. 'I was very careful – I wasn't followed, or recognized.' He gave a little chuckle. 'In fact, I was so well disguised, I stood next to Tanya and your mum – neither recognized me! Not a soul knew I was there.'

'Which match?' said Lee.

'Both.'

'*What!*'

'Charnley and Rotherhithe,' Dad grinned. 'I was there for them both. You and your teammates – I'm telling you – you *inspired* me.' He snapped his fingers. 'Fantastic football! *What a team!* That clinching goal against Charnley . . .?' He threw a playful punch to Lee's shoulder. '*Beauty!*'

Lee stared. Dad looked completely different – his skin had colour, he didn't just look neater, he looked . . .

healthy. He was acting differently – laughing, joking and relaxed . . . like his old self.

'I made a deal with Brian,' said Dad.

Brian was Dad's boss, the manager at his club.

'We've drawn up a new contract – official, signed and everything. We worked out how much I need for living expenses, paying the bills, money for Mum, Tanya and you, and so on – that amount is *all* I get paid. I won't get more till I score.'

'And what then?' said Lee.

'I'm on a minimum salary with a high goal-scoring bonus for the first ten goals . . .' Dad shrugged. 'After that, we re-negotiate. But listen – I'm *motivated* – the money isn't a factor . . . I'm not gambling.'

'So you're going to be playing?' said Lee.

'This is the deal – if I'm fit on the day, I might – only *might* – get to play. They won't make any announcements till just before the match. But if I'm fit, Brian's promised to consider me.' Dad made a clenched fist. 'I *know* I can do it . . . if they just give me the chance.'

Lee could scarcely believe it. This even *sounded* like the old Dad.

Dad leant in closer. 'Not a word of this to anybody, not even to Mum or your sister – understood? That's part of the deal. It has to be kept secret.'

Lee nodded. 'My lips are sealed.'

'Seeing Sunningdale,' said Dad, 'made me realize what I was missing. Enjoyment left the game for me, long before my injury. The years of pressure and distractions, the money, the constant attention and the lack of time and privacy for me to be with you . . . Mum . . . Tanya . . .' Dad shook his head. '. . . with all that stress and routine, it's so easy to lose sight of what's important. But watching you and your teammates, son, I suddenly saw it . . . I remembered what it was all about . . .'

Lee felt a smile spread across his lips.

But Dad's face was sombre. 'Lee – it won't ever be quite like before . . .'

'Good!'

Dad seemed puzzled by Lee's reaction. 'What I mean is: the glory days, Brooksie, the footballing genius . . .'

Lee swallowed. 'Dad . . .'

'I'm not going back on all I've just said,' Dad frowned. 'I *am* determined to get back in the thick of things . . .'

'Dad . . .'

'. . . all I'm saying is . . .'

'Soccer stars wear out and grow old?'

Dad's face flushed. He started to chuckle. 'What a cheek! I'm not saying I'm *past* it. If I'm picked and I get to play, I'll be out to show I'm still capable of *the best*. But . . . yeah – it's one of the things I've done a lot of thinking about: even if Brooksie gets back in there, he can't stay at the top for ever . . .'

Lee shrugged. 'I know. Everyone has to retire one day. But then you can become a coach or a manager.'

'For the time being, that's still the future!' Dad grinned and rubbed his hands. 'If I do get back in the team, I shan't be able to watch your final play-off . . . it'll be a shame to miss a game . . .'

'First match of the season . . .' said Lee. 'You're playing Man U!'

Ducking down behind the seat, Dad sat back up.

Lee stared. Dad now had *a beard*! *He was wearing a floppy sun hat*! Lee blinked. 'At the match – I've seen you on the sidelines!'

Dad nodded. 'Not just at the matches . . .' he chuckled. 'I was there at the *auction*! I'm now a collector of football memorabilia

193

and, for the time being young man, *I'm* going to be looking after this!'

'My signed football! The man in the hat!'

Dad grabbed him round the neck; half clinch, half embrace.

He hugged Dad's shoulder.

Dad grinned. Softly, he began to chant.

'. . . *Sunningdale United! Sunningdale United! Sunningdale United!'*

CHAPTER 20

Half-Time

The ref had to blow his whistle extra-hard for half-time. As the players left the pitch, they were barely able to hear themselves speak. The crowd was *loud*.

Lee grinned. It had been a non-stop first half. He had played some of his best football *ever*, and to cap it all – his last-minute goal had just put Sunningdale 2 – 1 ahead! It had been a long time since he'd felt this good.

Supporters from both sides were in an absolute frenzy.

'Nice one!' Roy's shout was close to Lee's ear.

'Look!' Dent pointed. '– talking to Jackson!'

Photographers! Instinctively, Lee lowered his head.

'Fame at last!' yelled Lurch.

The others laughed.

Lee dropped back. The two men with cameras were probably just from small local papers, but still . . . 'I'll catch up,' he said, 'I'm going to have a chat with Mum and Tanya.'

'Say – thanks!' Dent gestured towards a cluster of scarf-waving supporters. 'They've done a fantastic job!'

'Ditto!' yelled Roy.

Lee had seen Mum and Tanya standing with neighbours from the block, but now the crowd had begun to break up and move around, he'd lost sight of them. It was a mêlée.

Family and friends ran to players, offering congratulations, or words of encouragement; other supporters sat down to enjoy the sun. People milled about, they mingled and chatted to friends or made their way to join queues – one outside the Portaloo, three for ice-cream vans parked by the field.

A friendly pat on the back here, a cheer and a smile there – again and again, as he wove through the bustle, he smiled and nodded in return. Smiled and nodded, smiled and . . . *froze*.

Directly in front of him stood Tyler. His face looked darker and more twisted than ever.

'We meet again . . .' Tyler said, sharply. His smile was crooked, a lop-sided sneer. Tattooed muscles flexed beneath his string vest.

Lee stared.

To Tyler's left, Tubs looked hot and irritable. His huge arms were folded, his fat face flushed and sweating. Sky – eyes rolling, mouth twitching – blocked the other flank. Not a pretty bunch.

Tyler's grin twisted, like a knife in the back. 'We never had our little talk . . .'

Lee took a step. 'If you go anywhere *near* my sister . . .' The words blurted from his mouth. He jabbed a threatening finger towards Tyler.

Tyler's eyes narrowed. His teeth glinted in an evil grin. Throwing back his head, he howled with laughter.

Lee flinched.

Tubs and Sky grinned and bobbed with laughter too.

Lee stepped back.

Quick as a flash, Tyler lunged.

197

As Lee ducked, he felt a muscley arm clamp around his neck. The arm gripped like steel.

'*Steady!*' warned Tyler. Easy, boy, easy . . . don't get jumpy on us!' He yanked Lee upright and twisted his arm behind his back. '*Smile!*' he hissed.

People stared, then turned away.

Lee felt a shove in his back and stumbled forward.

'Somebody,' growled Tyler, 'wants a word. *Let's go!*'

The big man leant against a car. It wasn't the familiar sleek, black limousine, but some dirty massive jeep-thing. There was no suit this time, but heavy-looking boots. His bull head was freshly-clippered. His face showed no trace of sweat. He looked less official, but there was no doubting he meant business.

Tyler spoke into the big man's ear.

Lee stared. *Why were they picking on him?*

'Touching!' The big man chuckled. 'My son tells me you've been worried about your sister . . .'

Lee half-twitched, half-shrugged.

'Well, so you should be,' said the big

man, 'but not for the reasons you think.'

Tyler and his thugs seemed to find this amusing.

The big man smiled, the same lop-sided smile as his son. 'You've got the wrong idea about these lads,' he said, waving a hand in their direction, 'they're not your average thugs.'

Tyler and 'the lads' solemnly shook their heads.

'However . . .' said the big man, cracking his knuckles, '. . . they *do* support the national team, they *do* go to matches when England play at home and they *do* like the occasional laugh.'

The thugs nodded.

Lee bit his lip. *Where was this leading to?*

'A few weeks back,' said the big man, 'travelling home after a match – *would you believe it*? – my son and his mates came across a disgraced England soccer international . . .'

Tyler nodded. Lee's heart was racing. Suddenly he'd caught a glimpse of where this was leading. He tried to let nothing show.

'This player,' said the big man, 'has, on many occasions these past eighteen months, embarrassed himself, his club, his country and his family, with some of the most pathetic performances ever seen on pitch.' His eyes burned into Lee. *'Are you with me?'*

Lee's heart thumped so loudly, it seemed the big man should be shouting just to make himself heard. He nodded.

'Good,' said the big man. Now, when young Tyler spotted this alcoholic scumbag, this excuse-for-a-player, he was sitting with a little girl, eating in a pizza restaurant.'

Lee swallowed. *Tanya's story – the thugs outside the restaurant with the painted faces – Tyler and his gang! The big man knew! They all knew*!

'That little girl was Excuse-for-a-player's daughter,' said the big man. 'She has a brother. Excuse-for-a-player has a son – too ashamed to be seen out with his dad, I shouldn't wonder.' He leaned forward. 'Are you still following me?"

Lee was shaking. He forced himself to nod.

'Right now,' said the big man, 'in the place where the son is living, hardly a soul knows his true identity.' He stepped closer. 'What a waste it'd be, if the father's shame

were to blight the son's life for ever – eh?
But sadly, if word got out, that could very
easily happen . . .'

The big man glanced towards Tyler.
'. . . could it not?'

Tyler sneered and nodded.

'Now,' said the big man, '*we* can prevent
all that from happening. But in return, we
need the son's help with one little thing.'
He thrust the finger and thumb of his big
hand close to Lee's face. 'A *tiny* little thing
we need fixing . . .'

Lee forced a breath. 'What's that?'

'The match.'

CHAPTER 21

Full Time

Lee's head was spinning with the big man's words, as he hurried his way towards the team.

They sat or lay sprawled, a couple of them dutifully stretching their hamstrings.

Vinda was rubbing a bruised shin. 'Here he is!' he said, glancing up as Lee approached.

'We was worried you'd been nobbled,' chuckled Lurch.

'Or picked up by the talent scouts,' said Junior.

The others chuckled. *They* were in good spirits.

Lee rubbed the knot in his stomach. 'There was a queue for the Portaloo,' he said. It wasn't a lie. He winced.

'You're probably dehydrated,' said Roy. He chucked Lee a large bottle of watered-down juice. 'Get it down you, mate, the second half's about to start.'

'What's up with you?' said Dent. 'You'd better do something to get the colour back in your cheeks – the photographers heard you were here, so they're hanging about to get some snaps.'

Lee stared.

'Only kidding!' said Dent. 'There'll be team shots of the winners at full time.' He struck a victorious pose.

Lee tried to smile. 'Aren't you forgetting something?'

Dent frowned. 'What?'

'The second half.'

The others chuckled.

'Lee does look a funny colour!' said Junior.

'He never stopped running in the first half,' said Dent. He squinted at Lee. 'You're sure you're all right?'

Lee nodded and took a swig of the diluted orange.

'Your mum was looking for you.' Dent pointed. 'She's over with Jackson. Someone's got a radio. Everyone's listening to the footie.'

Lee turned to look.

Jackson, Mum and Tanya hovered on the fringes of a small crowd; the man in the centre held a transistor radio. Mum and Tanya waved.

'They kicked-off later than us, they're just coming up to half-time,' said Roy, 'And guess who's on the subs bench?'

'Brooksie?' said Lee.

'Yeah!' Lurch chuckled. 'Any minute now, the biggest joke in the Premier league could be stepping on to the pitch.'

'To take one more shot at embarrassing himself.' Dent spat at the ground.

Others tittered.

Lee gulped more orange. *Dad had got himself passed fit. They had to give him a chance. They had to!*

'Brooksie's last stand,' laughed Roy.

'Brooksie's last fall!' chuckled Vinda.

'Talking of jokes . . .' Lurch jumped to his feet.

The others groaned.

'Uh-oh!'

'Lurch is trying to be funny!'

'Go on.'

'Let's hear it . . .'

Lurch grinned. 'What's Brooksie's favourite position?'

'Face down on the pitch!'

'On his back – legs in the air!'

'You've heard it before!' Lurch laughed. The team laughed with him.

Lee felt sick. And *furious*. 'Brooksie's still got what it takes!' he snapped.

The laughter stopped. Heads turned.

'He'll *prove* it . . . if they just *give him the chance.*' His teammates stared. Lee pointed towards the pitch. 'Brooksie's not the only one with something to prove . . .'

'*SUNNINGDALE!*'

'GROVESNOR!'

'SUNNINGDALE!'

'GROVESNOR!'

The crowed roared and bayed.

Lee shook his head, despairingly. He'd blown it, *again*. It was all going wrong. On the touchline, Tyler, Tubs and Sky jumped and hooted, like jubilant gorillas.

Tyler's eyes watched him every step.

His muffed passes and bungled tackles had now led to two Grovesnor goals.

Sunningdale were 2 – 3 down!

'What are you playing at!' Dent was barely able to control his fury.

'Sorry . . .' Lee stared at the ground. Tyler and his dad probably thought he was doing what they'd demanded – fixing the match. He wasn't. He would never.

Dent was staring at him. 'Do you want me to bring on a sub?'

'No!'

'You're letting the side down!'

'Man on!' yelled Lee. 'Back to me, back to me! Come on – *back to me!*'

Dent tried to make a long pass, out to Lurch. It fell short.

Lee spat and ran after the ball. Dent no longer trusted him – and who could blame him? He had to win that trust back. Fast!

He accelerated. He chased.

The Grovesnor forward rolled and yelled, clutching his ankle, but Lee knew his tackle had been clean.

The ref signalled *play on*.

Yes! Lee sped away with the ball. The midfield were with him, tucked in behind;

the Grovesnors in their orange strip fell back. He looked for blue and gold.

Sunningdale! Sunningdale! Sunning-dale! Sunningdale!

The roar of the supporters carried him faster and faster.

He surged. He was a surfer on their wave!

Orange shirts turned to face him. They lunged.

Too late! He was a bolt of lightning!

He zig-zagged. He swerved, skipped and chipped past four. Unscathed.

The supporters went berserk.

Vinda was sailing deep on the left flank.

Dummying to the right, Lee doubled-back and lofted it over the remaining defenders.

Perfect – straight to Vinda's feet.

Lee glanced around. Anton, Jack and Junior were still behind him. Ahead, Dent and Sean were surrounded by defenders. Lurch, on the outside of the box, was trying to lose another two. There was a tunnel right down the middle. *This was it!*

Vinda's high pass was in the air and floating down over the heads.

The players in the box began jumping.

Lee sprinted. The roar was deafening! He was bowling into Grovesnor's heart, on a torrent of sound.

He timed it. Leapt. Got above it and *nutted* it, full-force . . .

SMACK into the back of the net.

'*YEEEEEEEEEES!*'

'*Sunn-ing-dale! Sunn-ing-dale! Sunn-ing-dale! Sunn-ing-dale!*'

'*Sunningdale U-ni-ted! Sunningdale U-ni-ted!*'

Disentangling himself from the net, Lee punched the air and grinned. *Confidence was back.*

'*Brooksie!*'

He jerked round, half-expecting a camera flash or . . .

'*What are you playing at?*'

It was the big man, just behind the goal. In amongst the crowd. His face was ballistic-red and quivering with rage.

He glared. 'Don't play games, you little piece of *scum!*'

'This is a pitch!' yelled Lee. 'That's what people do on pitches – they play games and they strive to *win!*'

Hands clapped him on the back.

'Wicked shot!'

Lee turned; Anton, Lurch and Dent were beaming.

'Sunningdale, Sunningdale – one – more – goal!'

Lee grinned. The wind had changed and Grovesnor were on the back foot. The equalizer had thrown them. There were only a few minutes to go, but Sunningdale could still do it!

Confidence is king.

When he chased the ball, he *knew* he would get it. When he passed, he *knew* it would go where he intended. If he called, the pass came.

The referee checked his watch.

Lee had the ball at his feet.

'Come *on*, Sunningdale!' yelled Dent. 'Let's do this without penalties!'

Lee was running. Dent, four metres ahead to his left, glanced back.

Orange shirts swooped.

Lee passed to Dent last minute and, dodging a clumsy tackle, sprinted ahead. Dent repeated in reverse. The timing was perfect.

The supporters loved it.

'Sunningdale, Sunningdale – one – more – goal! Sunningdale, Sunningdale – one – more – goal!'

Lee slowed a little, dancing with the ball.

Dent raced past, flashing a smile and found a gap.

Flicking the ball up and over, Lee ducked through the middle of three defenders and raced after it. *Cheeky!*

Twisting to avoid collision with another defender, he took off to the right.

Dent was on the edge of the box. Junior, Sean and Anton were in it. Lurch coming fast on the right. Vinda struggling to shake off his shadows on the left.

Lee hooked the ball to Lurch and changed tack.

From now on in, it had to be one-touch.

Lurch headed to Dent.

Dent lofted wide.

Vinda streaked in, leapt above three weary defenders and nodded it straight up in the air.

Lee glanced at the magic spot – top left – between crossbar and post.

Running in, barging down the middle, everything seemed to happen in slow motion. The sound was deafening.

Head down, he whacked the falling ball
on the volley.
'GOAL!'
It was there!
The whistle blew. And blew again.

CHAPTER 22

Endgame

They had won! They were through! They were being mobbed by their home crowd.

Lee was grinning like every Sunningdale player and supporter around him.

Cheers, handshakes, claps on the back . . . He felt *dazed*. The full force of the supporters' enthusiasm was over-whelming.

Excited, but exhausted, the players were pulled this way and that.

Lee tried to clutch an arm, but missed. He was being separated from the rest of the team; he was being sucked along by a sea of adoring fans. He tried to push against the crush, he tried to dig in his heels, he was being dragged . . .

Crashing into something solid, Lee looked up.

Snarling mouth . . . flaring nostrils . . . livid eyes . . .

The big man.

'Ow!' Lee winced. Someone was twisting his arm.

He turned.

Tyler leered and twisted again.

'Ow!'

Tyler yanked his arm, Tubs grabbed hold from the other side. Sky grinned insanely.

'Enjoy these last few minutes,' snarled the big man, 'because *you* . . .' he jabbed a finger into Lee's shoulder, '. . . are about to be publicly humiliated, *Brooksie!*'

Lee winced again. The big man's breath stank horribly – a stench like rotten potatoes. He felt the big man's saliva on his cheek. Gasping for breath, he stared into the heavy-lidded eyes. 'You can't hurt me,' he said.

'You don't think so?' snorted the big man.

Lee shook his head. He wasn't trembling. He could actually feel himself smiling.

The big man's eyes bulged. His forehead furrowed. *'We'll see . . .'*

'I'm stone,' said Lee.

The puzzled frown deepened. The big man glowered. His red face turned purple, *dark* purple.

Tyler yanked Lee close and snarled in his ear. 'You're done for!' he growled.

Lee held the big man's gaze, determined not to blink. 'I'm stone,' he repeated.

The big man's nostrils flared. He turned to Tyler. *'Come on!'* he snapped, '– we've a public announcement to make and a family to expose.'

Tyler pushed Lee to Tubs. Nearly crushing him with his arms, Tubs pushed him to Sky. Sky leered.

'Leave him!' snapped the big man. 'Come on!'

The big man turned and stormed off through the crowd, pushing and barging people out of his way. Tubs, Tyler and Sky followed in his wake.

Lee shivered. Stone! *Who was he trying to kid!* Suddenly, his knees were shaking . . . he was laughing, his whole body was shaking. Stone indeed! He felt closer to jelly than stone.

'Lee!'

Lee spotted Roy's gappy grin.

'Roy!'

The rest of the team were there . . . Anton, Sean, Jack and Dent . . . being carried along by the movement of the crowd.

Roy reached towards him, between a couple of jumping, chanting supporters.

Lee grabbed his arm and pulled.

Vinda was there. Lurch and Junior behind him.

Roy laughed. 'All right, mate?'

Lee nodded. 'Still a bit queasy.'

'Exhaustion,' said Vinda. 'You need some air.'

Lee clutched Roy's shoulder. 'How about a ride?' he said.

'No problem!' Roy grinned. 'I've bags of strength – I've been loafing around in the goalmouth since the equalizer.' He dropped to his knees.

From up on Roy's shoulders, Lee could see everything. Jackson was struggling to set up a microphone stand. The Portakabin steps were being prepared as a mini-stage for the announcement of the result.

A couple of metres away, Dent popped up on someone else's shoulders. He waved and called out to Lee, then shouted directions to his carrier. The crowd swept them and the rest of the team along in the direction of the Portakabin.

Lee scanned the sea of heads. In front, pushing their way through the crowd and nearing the steps, he spotted the big man with his escort of thugs. The big man was waving and shouting.

From the Portakabin doorway, Jackson nodded and gestured to the big man. People moved out of the big man's way.

Suddenly, the cheering and shouting dropped.

Lee looked around. The crowd was breaking into clusters. People were gathering around the few who were carrying transistor radios. A whisper spread through the crowd. There were whoops. There were jeers. A muffled laugh. Then *hush* . . .

'They're putting him on!' yelled someone.

'Brooksie's going to play!' yelled another.

Lee felt shivers trembling up and down his spine. He glanced at his watch. There could only be a few minutes of the match left. Dad was being given a chance after all. But not much of one!

He crossed his fingers and bit his lip.

Everywhere there were surprised gasps

of 'Brooksie'. Some people were laughing, some were jeering. But everyone was listening.

Dent stared over the heads.

Lee stared back. He shrugged.

The makeshift loudspeaker system kicked into life with a high-pitched feedback screech. Jackson tapped the microphone. 'We're very lucky to have here with us today, the secretary of the southeast region of the Sunday Afternoon League – Mr Thomson.'

Sporadic outbreaks of clapping faded quickly.

A portly man, a little too wide for his summer suit, swept back a fringe of white hair, adjusted his spectacles and coughed into the microphone. 'Good afternoon!'

The crowd stared.

'Today's match was an immensely entertaining one, I think you'll all agree. Both sides displayed tremendous skill, courage, stamina and teamwork.' He peered over the top of his spectacles at the crowd.

Lee looked about. The crowd were watching the man at the microphone, but everyone's attention was on the radio football commentary.

'In my capacity as secretary,' said Mr

Thomson, 'over the years, I have been lucky enough to witness more local matches than most – at *all* ages and levels. And I have to say – I cannot remember such an exciting under-fourteens game.'

Mr Thomson cleared his throat.

'Nor can I *ever* remember attending a local league fixture that has been so well attended. It is *quite incredible*. Supporters and teams – you have done yourselves proud!'

The audience barely managed a half-hearted cheer.

Mr Thomson looked perplexed. 'It gives me great pleasure,' he hurried on, 'to announce the winners of today's final play-off – Sunningdale United . . .'

This time there was scarcely a murmur from the crowd.

Lee tapped Roy's head. 'What's happening?'

'Two–all!'

The loudspeaker crackled.

'Sunningdale,' said Mr Thomson, 'will be taking their place in the Sunday Afternoon League's south-east region, under-fourteens division. Their first match will be in three weeks time. Carry on supporting them! This promises to be a jolly exciting season . . .'

'*It's Brooksie with the ball!*' yelled a voice from the crowd.

'*He's on the run!*' yelled another.

Lee's heart leapt up his throat.

On the Portakabin steps, Jackson stepped up to the microphone. 'One of our local representatives,' he said, 'Councillor Tyler, has requested the opportunity to say a few words.'

Lee swallowed and took a deep breath.

With some awkwardness, the big man and Jackson shuffled places on the tiny impromptu stage. The big man stared across the heads of the crowd. His eyes locked on Lee.

Beneath Lee, Roy jerked and twisted. 'Oi, watch it!' he yelled, 'you'll pull my ears off.'

'Ladies and gentlemen . . .' The big man's boomy voice rattled the small loudspeaker.

'*Shhhhhh!*' The crowd hissed loudly. Nothing could be allowed to interrupt the last few moments of the big match.

Clutching the microphone stand, the big man seemed to stumble. He looked shaken.

A hand thrust a radio up above the

crowd. *'It's Brooksie,'* yelled a voice, *'it's Brooksie . . . all the way!'*

The hush became a buzz of excitement.

'Brooksie!' It was Dent's voice shouting. *'Come on, Brooksie!'*

'Go on, Brooksie!' yelled someone else.

'You can do it, mate!' called another voice.

'He's running through them all!'

'He's inside the penalty area . . .'

'SHOOOOOT!' yelled Lee.

There was a momentary hush as everyone held their breath. Tiny tinny voices squeaked from transistor radios. Then – the whole crowd *erupted*. It was a *ROAR*.

'He's SCORED!' went up the cry. *'Brooksie's gone and done it!'*

Yells, whistles, cheers and shouts – suddenly everybody was leaping and laughing, punching the air and waving their arms.

'Brook-sie! Brook-sie! Brook-sie! Brook-sie!'

Lee clung to Roy's head. He felt like he was going to *explode* with happiness.

Roy, seeming to have forgotten his passenger altogether, jumped and jigged about with the rest of them.

'Goal! Goal! Goal!' shouted the crowd. *'Brooksie's back! Brooksie's back!'*

On the steps of the Portakabin, the big man was staring in shock. He cleared his throat into the microphone. 'I'd just like to make an . . . er . . .'

The big man could barely be heard behind the chanting of the crowd. The loudspeaker made a high-pitched screeching feedback noise, as it was turned up to full capacity.

The big man tried again. *'Ladies and gentlemen . . .'*

'Shhhhhhhhhh . . .'

The crowd begin to simmer down.

'. . . this ground,' said the big man, 'on which the two teams have been playing today has, for a long time now, been the subject of . . . erm . . . development plans. However, I would like, here and now, to make public my undertaking that this pitch, or another like it *will* be made available for the boys of Sunningdale United to practise on . . .' The big man had to cough to clear his throat. '. . . to play on,' he croaked, '. . . and *win* on.'

The Sunningdale supporters whooped and roared, the Grovesnor fans applauded.

Up on Roy's jerking, bouncing shoulders, Lee yelled himself hoarse.

On the steps, next to Jackson, he could see Mum waving and wiping a tear. Jackson hoisted Tanya up to to his hip, so she could wave too.

He waved back for all he was worth.

Mum's magic smile beamed across the crowd like a beacon.

Over to his side, Dent was waving his arms and roaring with the crowd.

'Brook-sie!'

'Sunning-dale!'

'Brook-sie!'

'He's my dad!' yelled Lee.

Dent grinned and nodded back.

Could he hear? It didn't matter . . .

Lee punched the air and joined the chant.

'Sunning-dale!'

'Brook-sie!'

'Sunning-dale!'

'Brook-sie!'

THE END

FOOTBALL MAGIC!
E. Dale

The competition's really tough – everyone wants to go on Football Magic!

Andy, Paul and Leroy are the best soccer players in their schools. That's why they're on the Football Magic course. But what is a wimpy looking boy like Dave doing there? He's not like the rest of them. He doesn't boast about his talents for a start. AND he keeps sticking up for girls. Just because his sister scored the winning goal in the Inter-Schools Cup, doesn't mean girls are any good at football, does it?

But Dave has something to prove, and once he gets on the pitch his skills do all the talking. He's magic! But what will everyone think when they learn his secret?

End-to-end action on and off the pitch in this great soccer story!

0 440 863589

CORGI YEARLING BOOKS

SOCCER MAD
Rob Childs

'This is going to be the match of the century!'

Luke Crawford is crazy about football. A
walking encyclopedia of football facts and
trivia, he throws his enthusiasm into being
captain of the Swillsby Swifts, a Sunday
team made up mostly of boys like himself
– boys who love playing football but get
few chances to play in real matches.

Luke is convinced that good teamwork and
plenty of practice can turn his side into
winners on the pitch, but he faces a real
challenge when the Swifts are drawn to
play the Padley Panthers – the league
stars – in the first round of the
Sunday League Cup . . .

0 440 863589

CORGI YEARLING BOOKS